RILKE was born in Prague in 1875, the son of a conventional army-officer father and a religious-fanatical mother, who first sent him, most unsuitably, to military school. After that, largely autodidact, he studied philosophy, history, literature, art, in Prague, Munich, Berlin. From his earliest years he wrote verse. In the '90s both *Erste* and *Frühe Gedichte* appeared, short stories, plays. Much of his early work he declined to include in his collected works. In 1899 (which saw the *Cornet*, first version) came the first of two trips to Russia with Lou Andreas-Salomé (*Vom lieben Gott und Anderes,* later to be called *Geschichten vom Lieben Gott,* appeared in December 1900). He married Clara Westhoff in 1901, lived in Worpswede till the birth of their only child, Ruth, moving to Paris in 1902, Clara to work with Rodin, Rilke to write his monograph on him. Between travels in Germany, France, Italy, Spain, Egypt, Scandinavia, and his prodigious letter-writing, the twelve years with Paris as base were productive: *Stundenbuch, Buch der Bilder, Neue Gedichte, Notebooks of M. L. Brigge,* translations of E. B. Browning, Gide, de Guérin. After the outbreak of World War I he lived mostly in Munich, served briefly in army office work in Vienna, and in 1919 went to Switzerland. Here, in the small stone tower of Muzot, he achieved in 1922 the *Duineser Elegien* and the *Sonette an Orpheus,* followed by poems in French and translations of Valéry and others. He died at Valmont near Glion on December 29, 1926, and is buried beside the little church of Raron overlooking the Rhone Valley.

RAINER MARIA RILKE

In Translations by M. D. HERTER NORTON
Letters to a Young Poet
Sonnets to Orpheus
Wartime Letters to Rainer Maria Rilke
Translations from the Poetry of Rainer Maria Rilke
The Lay of the Love and Death of Cornet Christopher Rilke
The Notebooks of Malte Laurids Brigge
Stories of God

Translated by STEPHEN SPENDER and J. B. LEISHMAN
Duino Elegies

Translated by JANE BANNARD GREENE and M. D. HERTER NORTON
Letters of Rainer Maria Rilke
Volume One, 1892–1910   Volume Two, 1910–1926

Translated by DAVID YOUNG
Duino Elegies

In Various Translations
Rilke on Love and Other Difficulties
Translations and Considerations of Rainer Maria Rilke
Compiled by JOHN J. L. MOOD

STORIES OF

*G*OD

❧

Rainer Maria Rilke

Translation by M. D. Herter Norton

W · W · NORTON & COMPANY

New York · London

Library of Congress Catalog Card No. 63–11685

ISBN 0-393-30882-0

W. W. Norton & Company, Inc.
500 Fifth Avenue, New York, N. Y. 10110
W. W. Norton & Company Ltd
10 Coptic Street, London WC1A 1PU

≫≪

My FRIEND, *I once gave this book into your hands, and you cared for it as no one had yet done. So I have grown accustomed to think that it belongs to you. Suffer me, therefore, not only in your own book but in all the books of this new edition to write your name; to write:*

The STORIES OF GOD *belong to*
ELLEN KEY

RAINER MARIA RILKE
Rome, April 1904

Contents

Translator's Note

❧

> ". . . these youthful fantasies were almost entirely
> improvised out of an instinct which, if I were to
> specify it more particularly, I might describe as busied
> with transferring God from the sphere of rumor into
> the realm of direct and daily experiencing; the rec-
> ommending by every means a naïve and lively taking-
> into-use of God with which I seemed to have been
> charged since childhood. . . ."

BEYOND this, written twenty years later by a poet who
disliked attempting to explain how he had come to write a
particular work and usually fell back on the idea of some
subconscious or automatic dictation, we know little of the
genesis of the *Stories of God*. None of the manuscript
material has survived. They obviously come after Rilke's
first Munich days, his early experiences of Italy and his first
Russian journey in the spring of 1899.

According to other statements of his own, Rilke was
fond of this book, the thirteen tales of which he had written
down—in a manner so characteristic of his working—at a
happy moment somewhere between the 10th and the 21st
of November, 1899, in the course of seven consecutive
nights. It first appeared just before Christmas 1900, but un-

der a different title, namely *Vom lieben Gott und Anderes/ an Grosse für Kinder erzählt* (*Of God and Other Matters/ told to Grownups for Children*). The roundabout approach implied in the subtitle was meant to cover the embarrassment he always sensed on talking with children, to which he refers in the introductory tale. Though he felt how truly the wide and real world belongs to "young youth", this constraint made spontaneous communication impossible, so that only by some such device as this could he reach those who he knew would understand him if he "tried to say something about God". The little artifice, thus charmingly accounted for, remains an ingredient of the story-telling, but when in the following year Insel-Verlag brought out a second impression of the book it was under the present title, *Geschichten vom lieben Gott*, the subtitle dropped.

In 1904 the publishers expressed a wish to scrap the old format—which Rilke had never liked: "unhandy and unpretty", he called it—in favor of a simpler and more attractive volume; and for this (properly speaking) second edition he revised the text during February and March of that year, in Rome. The alterations were fairly numerous, but slight, involving single words, some phrases, some points of punctuation, but the style of the writing remained unchanged. At Rilke's own request his friend and admirer Ellen Key, the Swedish feminist, had prepared a brief foreword for it. But, though this had already been set by the printer, when Rilke saw it he changed his mind: it tried too hard to interpret, reading thoughts expressed in later letters back into this work of four years ago, offering keys to all its doors, whereas, since everything in it was presentiment, anticipation both fearful and joyful, it could not endure so much light cast upon it: "it must be alone with itself". The foreword never appeared, therefore; instead there is the dedication to Ellen Key.

Despite his kindly sentiments towards this early work, when the first edition of his *Collected Works* (*Gesammelte Werke*) was being planned in 1925 Rilke wrote his publisher that he did not like the idea of his "youthful pre-prose (which was not yet prose)" being included in the volume with the *Notebooks of Malte Laurids Brigge;* unless perhaps the monograph on Rodin followed it, acting as a bridge between the two larger prose works. It came out in Volume IV, with *Prose Fragments* and the *Rodin.* Now, finally, it stands in Volume IV (1961) of the definitive *Complete Works* (*Sämtliche Werke*), together with sundry early stories and plays.

In its second form (1904) the book has never been out of print. It went through twelve impressions in Rilke's lifetime and has been translated into various languages besides English: French, Spanish, Italian, Dutch, Swedish, Polish, Czechish. The present English translation—a revision of its predecessor, in the groundwork of which the translator had the benefit of collaborating with the late Countess Nora Purtscher-Wydenbruck, a niece of that good friend of Rilke's, Princess Marie of Thurn and Taxis—is, of course, based on the text as it now stands in the *Complete Works.*

Even if by his own more mature standards this text represents "pre-prose", it is such characteristic Rilke that in the light of experience the translation has deserved revision in considerable detail. The mode of expression, in itself not unique for the period in any literature—on purpose slightly stilted at times, with its touches of humor, of irony, its stylized whimsy, its biblical turns to rouse an echo of familiar phraseology—must still be kept, quite as much as the poetic qualities of concept and description which are the distinguishing features of a great artist's accomplishment. Translating Rilke means translating not only German—and to begin with, we have no satisfactory way of rendering *"vom lieben Gott"*—but Rilke's very individual German. He sometimes uses odd words; more often he uses words oddly; sometimes he invents words, a process which goes better in German than in English. Nine times out of ten one discovers an acuteness of observation and intent in his peculiar employment of a tense, an adjective, an adverb, a preposition. These items are easily overlooked in the mechanics of translation; one must be constantly on guard, balancing between too-literal adherence to an unusual expression and the expected commonplace, at all costs avoiding indifference to genuine distinctions.

Autobiographical elements will naturally be recognized in the writing by anyone at all familiar with Rilke's works, letters and early diaries. Here and there touches of local color in implied references to customs and conventions of his own young days also occur as part of the background. Whether Rilke's allusions to Renaissance history and art show a thoroughly disciplined knowledge or not; whether, as has been suggested, his fascination with Russia sprang largely from what he himself felt and wanted to recognize in it; whether for all his love and enthusiasm for that country he makes some mistakes in his Russian or mixes up his heroes or interprets folktales in his own way—these points are not in question here. They have been ably dealt with elsewhere. We take the background material of these stories as it was intended, for its atmospheric value. A few indications relevant to sources and expressions are touched upon in the *Notes* at the end of the volume.

The writer of a foreword may consider it his task to expound upon what he thinks his author means by what he will be saying in the coming pages. A translator's note will be most usefully confined to some more modest comment on the work in hand, but it should certainly convey its perpetrator's apologies for offering something that by the nature of its case can never be wholly satisfactory. For better or worse, the translator's understanding is conveyed in the result of his effort, and interpretations, preliminary or subsequent, seem uncalled-for: though unfortunately at one remove from the original, the reader now takes over and will make his own guesses. This book of stories is the youthful work of a great poet. It should be read and enjoyed "alone with itself".

M.D.H.N.

Whitherton on Shadow Lane
Wilton, Connecticut
November 1962

STORIES OF GOD

The Tale
of the Hands of God

❧

RECENTLY, one morning, I met the lady who lives next door. We exchanged greetings.

"What an autumn!" she exclaimed after a pause, and looked up at the sky. I did the same. The morning was indeed very clear and exquisite for October.

Suddenly I had an idea. "What an autumn!" I cried, waving about a little with my hands. And my neighbor nodded in assent. I watched her thus for a moment. Her good, healthy face bobbed up and down so amiably. It was very bright, only around the lips and at the temples there were little shadowy wrinkles. How could she have got them? And then I asked, all unexpectedly: "And your little girls?"

The wrinkles in her face vanished for a second, but gathered again at once, darker than before. "Well thank God; but——"; my neighbor began to walk on, and I now strode along at her left as is proper.

"You know, they have both reached the age, those children, when they *ask* all day long. 'What'—all day long, and right straight into the night."

"Yes," I murmured, "there is a time . . ."

But she took no notice.

"And not just questions such as: Where does this horse-car go? How many stars are there? And is ten thousand more than many? Quite different things as well! For example: Does God speak Chinese too? and: What does God look like? Always everything about God! But that's something we ourselves don't know about—"

"No, of course—" I agreed, "though we can have our guesses . . ."

"Or about God's hands—what is one to—"

I looked my neighbor full in the face. "Pardon me," said I most politely, "you just said the hands of God, did you not?"

She nodded. I think she was a little surprised.

"Well," I hastened to add, "I happen to know something about those hands. By chance," I remarked quickly, as I saw her eyes grow round, "quite by chance—I— — well", I finished with considerable decision, "I will tell you what I know. If you have a moment, I will accompany you to your house; that will just give me time."

"Gladly," said she, when at last I let her speak, still much astonished, "but wouldn't you like . . .?"

"To tell the children myself? No, dear lady, that wouldn't do, that wouldn't do at all. You see, I promptly get embarrassed when I have to talk with children. That in itself is not bad. But the children might think I was embarrassed because I felt myself telling lies. . . . And as the veracity of my story is very important to me—why, you can repeat it to the children; you will surely do it much better. You can put it together and embellish it; I will just give you the simple facts in the shortest form. Shall I?"

"Very well, very well," said my neighbor absently.

I reflected: "In the beginning—," but I broke off at once. "I may assume that you, my dear neighbor, already know many of the things that I would first have to tell the children. For example, about the creation . . ."

There was a considerable pause.

"Yes—and on the seventh day . . ." The good woman's voice was high and sharp.

"Stop!" I cried. "We must think of the earlier days too; for indeed it is they that concern us. Well, God, as we know, began his work by making the earth, distinguishing it from the waters, and decreeing light. Then he fashioned, with amazing rapidity, things—I mean the big real things that are: rocks, mountains, a tree and after this pattern many trees."

Now I had for some time been hearing footsteps behind us, which neither caught up to us nor fell back. That bothered me, and I became entangled in my story of the creation as I went on in the following manner: "One can only arrive at an understanding of this swift and fruitful activity if one assumes that after long and deep reflection everything must have been all ready in his head before he . . ."

Now at last the footsteps were beside us, and a not exactly pleasant voice fastened itself upon us: "Oh, surely you are speaking of Herr Schmidt, pardon me. . ."

I looked at the newcomer with annoyance, but my companion became very much embarrassed. "Ahem," she coughed, "no—that is—yes,—we were just speaking, in a way . . ."

"What an autumn!" said the other woman suddenly, as though nothing had happened, and her red little face beamed.

"Yes," I heard my neighbor reply, "you are right, Frau Hüpfer, an exceptionally fine autumn."

Then the ladies parted. Frau Hüpfer tittered on: "And give the little children my love." My good neighbor took no more notice; of course she was curious to hear my story. I, however, declared with incomprehensible asperity: "Yes, but *now* I've forgotten where we stopped."

"You were just saying something about his head—that is—" My neighbor turned scarlet.

I was truly sorry for her, so I quickly went on: "Well, you see as long as only *things* were being made, God did not need to look down on the earth continually. Nothing could happen there. The wind was, indeed, already moving among the mountains, which were so like the clouds it had long known, but it still shunned the trees with a certain mistrust. And that was quite right with God. *Things* he had fashioned so to speak in his sleep, and only when he came to the animals did the work begin to interest him; he bent over it and only seldom raised his broad brows to cast a glance down at the earth. He forgot it completely when he began to create man. I don't know which complicated part of the body he had arrived at, when there was a rush of wings about him. An angel hurried by, singing: 'Thou who seest all . . .'

God started. He had caused that angel to sin, for it was

a lie he had just sung. Quickly God-the-Father peered down. And sure enough, something had already happened that was hardly to be remedied. A little bird was fluttering hither and yon over the earth, as though it were frightened, and God was in no position to help it home, for he had not seen out of *which* forest the poor creature had come. He grew very vexed and said: 'The birds are to sit still where I put them.' But then he remembered that at the request of the angels he had lent them wings, so that on earth too there would be something like angels, and this circumstance annoyed him even more. Now in such a state of mind nothing is so salutary as work. And busied with the construction of man, God quickly grew happy again. He had the eyes of the angels before him as mirrors, measured his own features in them, and was slowly and carefully modeling, on a ball in his lap, the first face. He had succeeded with the forehead. Much more difficult for him was making the two nostrils symmetrical. He bent lower and lower over the work, till a wind passed over him again; he looked up. The same angel was circling around him; no hymn was to be heard this time, for with his lie the boy's voice had been extinguished, but God could see by his mouth that he was still singing: 'Thou who seest all. . .'

At that moment Saint Nicholas, who stands especially high in God's esteem, came up to him and said through his big beard: 'Your lions are sitting quite still, and very haughty beasts they are, I must say. But a little dog is running round on the very edge of the world, a terrier, see, he'll be falling off in a moment.'

And indeed, God noticed a little bright speck, white,

like a tiny light, dancing about in the neighborhood of Scandinavia, where the earth is already so fearfully round. And he was exceedingly angry and reproachfully told Saint Nicholas, if he didn't like his lions, he should try and make some himself. Whereat Saint Nicholas walked out of heaven and slammed the door so hard that a star fell down, right on the terrier's head. Now the mischief was done, and God had to admit to himself that it was all his own fault; and he determined not to take his eyes off the earth any more. And so it was. He left the work to his hands, which of course are wise themselves, and although he was extremely curious to find out what man might look like, he continued to gaze fixedly down at the earth, where now, as if out of spite, not a leaflet would stir. To have at least some little pleasure after all this trouble, he had bidden his hands to show him man first before they should deliver him over to life. Repeatedly he asked, as children ask when they play hide-and-seek, 'Ready?' But for answer he heard the kneading of his hands and he waited. It seemed very long to him.

Then suddenly he saw something falling through space, something dark and in a direction that made it seem to come from quite near him. Filled with evil foreboding, he called to his hands. They appeared, all blotched with clay, hot and trembling.

'Where is man?' God thundered at them.

The right hand flew at the left: 'You dropped him!'

'Excuse me,' countered the left, provoked, 'you insisted on doing everything by yourself, you wouldn't even let me have anything to say.'

'But you ought to have held him!' And the right hand

drew back as if to strike, but then thought better of it, and the two raced each other in saying:

'He was so impatient, man. He was in such a hurry to live. It is not our fault; really, we are both innocent.'

But God was seriously angry. He pushed both hands away, for they blocked the earth from his sight. 'I've finished with you from now on; go and do as you like!'

And that is what his hands have been trying to do ever since, but whatever they start, they can only *begin*. Without God there is no perfection. And so at last they tired of it. Now they are on their knees all day long, doing penance —at least, so it is said. To us, however, it appears as though God were resting, because he is angry with his hands. It is still the seventh day."

I was silent for a moment. My companion used that moment very sensibly: "And do you think they will never again be reconciled?"

"Oh, yes," I said. "At least I hope so."

"And when might that be?"

"Well, not until God knows what man, whom his hands released against his will, looks like."

My neighbor reflected, then said with a laugh: "But for that all he needed would have been to look down . . ."

"Pardon me," said I politely, "your remark shows acumen, but my story is not yet done. You see, when his hands had got out of the way and God looked over the earth again, another instant—or, rather, a thousand years, which is of course the same thing—had gone by. Instead of *one* man, there were already a million. But then, too, they were all already wearing clothes. And as the fashion was very ugly at that time and even distorted people's faces badly, God received an entirely false and (I will not conceal the fact) a very poor impression of mankind."

"Hm," said my neighbor, about to make some remark. I took no notice, but concluded with great emphasis:

"And that is why it is urgently necessary that God should learn what man really is like. Let us rejoice that there are those who tell him . . ."

The good lady was not yet rejoicing.

"And who might they be, if you please?"

"Simply the children, and now and again, too, the people who paint, write poems, build . . ."

"Build what, churches?"

"Yes, and other things too—build in general . . ."

My neighbor slowly shook her head. Parts of my story seemed to her very remarkable. We had already gone past her house and now turned slowly about. Suddenly she exclaimed with a merry laugh:

"But what nonsense, for of course God is omniscient! He must have known, for example, exactly where the little bird had come from." She looked at me triumphantly.

I was rather taken aback, I must confess. But when I had recovered my composure, I managed a perfectly serious expression. "My dear lady," I informed her, "that is really a story in itself. But lest you think this merely an excuse on my part" [naturally, she now protested warmly], "I will briefly explain. God has *all* the attributes, of course. But before he was in a position to exercise them—as it were —upon the world, they all seemed to him like a single great force. I don't know whether I make myself clear. But in confronting things, his faculties became specialized and turned, to a certain degree, into duties. He had difficulty remembering everything. There are always conflicts. (Incidentally, all this I am telling to you alone, and you must on no account retell it to the children.)"

"Oh, I wouldn't dream of it," my listener declared.

"You see, if an angel had flown by him singing: 'Thou who *knowest* all,' everything would have come right . . ."

"And there would have been no need for this story?"

"Exactly," I confirmed. And I prepared to take my leave.

"But are you absolutely certain about all this?"

"I am absolutely certain," I replied almost solemnly.

"Then I shall have plenty to tell the children to-day!"

"I should love to be able to listen. Good-bye."

"Good-bye," answered my neighbor.

Then she turned back again. "But why did that particular angel . . ."

"My dear neighbor," said I, interrupting her, "I now see that your two dear little girls ask so many questions not at all because they are children . . ."

"But—?" she asked inquisitively.

"Well, the doctors say there are certain hereditary traits . . ."

My neighbor shook her finger at me. But we nevertheless parted the best of friends.

* *

*W*HEN I met my good neighbor again later (after a considerable interval, indeed), she was not alone, so I could not ask her whether she had acquainted her little girls with my story, and with what success. But my doubts upon that matter were dispelled by a letter I received soon afterwards. As I have not obtained permission from the sender of this letter to publish it, I must confine myself to telling how it ended, whence without further ado you will see from whom it came. It closed with the words: "I and still five other children, to wit, because I count myself one of them."

I answered, by return of post, as follows:

"My dear children, I well understand your liking the tale of the hands of God; I like it too. But all the same, I cannot come to see you. Do not take it amiss. Who knows whether you would like me? I have an ugly nose, and if, as sometimes happens, it also has a tiny red pimple at the tip, you would stare at that little point the whole time and be astonished and would not even hear what I was saying a little lower down. And you would probably dream of that little pimple. All that wouldn't suit me at all. Therefore I suggest another way out of the difficulty. We have (even without your mother) a lot of friends and acquaintances in common who are *not* children. You will soon find out who they are. To them I will tell a story from time to time, and from these intermediaries you will receive it in a form still more beautiful than that which I might have been able to give it. For indeed there are some great poets among these our friends. I shall not tell you what my stories will be about. But as I know that nothing is closer to your minds and hearts than God, I shall bring in at every suitable opportunity whatever I know about him. If anything isn't correct, write me another nice letter or let me know through your mother. For it is possible I might make a mistake here and there, because it is already so long since I have heard the nicest stories, and because since then I have had to remember a lot that are not so nice. That is the way it happens in life. But all the same, life is something perfectly glorious: of that too my stories will often speak. With love—I, who am one too, but only because I count myself one of you."

The Stranger

❧

A STRANGER has written me a letter. Not of Europe has the stranger written me, nor of Moses, nor of the great or the small prophets, not of the Emperor of Russia, nor of the Tsar, Ivan the Terrible, his dreadful ancestor. Not of the mayor or of our neighbor the cobbler, not of the nearby town, not of the far towns; and even the forest with the many deer, in which I lose myself every morning, is not mentioned in his letter. He tells me nothing either about his dear mama or about his sisters, who have probably married long ago. Perhaps his dear mama is dead; how else could it be that in a four-page letter I find her nowhere mentioned! He shows a much, much greater confidence in me; he makes me his brother, he tells me of his need.

In the evening the stranger comes to see me. I light no lamp, I help him off with his coat and beg him to drink tea with me, for it is just the hour at which I daily drink my tea. And on such intimate visits one need feel no constraint. As we are about to sit at table, I notice that my guest is restless; his face is full of anxiety and his hands tremble. "Oh, yes," say I, "here is a letter for you." And then I begin to pour the tea. "Do you take sugar? And lemon perhaps? In Russia I learned to drink tea with lemon. Will you

try?" Then I light a lamp, and place it in a far corner, rather
high, so that twilight really remains in the room, only a
somewhat warmer twilight than before, a rosy twilight. And
therewith my guest's face too seems more certain, warmer
and by far more familiar.

I welcome him once more with the words: "You know,
I have been expecting you for a long while." And before
the stranger has time to be astonished, I explain: "I know
a story which I can tell no one but you; do not ask me why,
only tell me whether your chair is comfortable, whether
the tea is sweet enough and whether you want to hear the
story."

My guest had to smile. Then he said simply: "Yes."

"To all three questions: yes?"

"To all three."

We both leaned back at the same moment in our chairs
so that our faces became shadowy. I put my tea-glass down,
rejoiced at the golden glint of the tea, slowly forgot this joy
again and asked suddenly: "Do you still remember God?"

The stranger reflected. His eyes looked deep into the
dark, and with the little points of light in the pupils they
resembled two long arbored walks in a park, over which
summer and sun lie luminous and broad. These too begin
so, with round twilight, stretching in ever narrowing ob-
scurity back to a distant, shimmering point—the exit on
the far side into a perhaps much brighter day. While I was
realizing this, he said, hesitating and as though he were
only reluctantly using his voice: "Yes, I still remember
God."

"Good," I thanked him, "for it is with him that my

story deals. But first tell me, do you sometimes talk to children?"

"Well, it does happen, just in passing, at least—"

"Perhaps you know that God, in consequence of some horrid disobedience of his hands, does not know what a finished man really looks like?"

"I heard that once somewhere, but I can't recall from whom—" my guest replied, and I saw uncertain memories fleeting across his brow.

"No matter," I broke in, "listen to the story:

A long time God endured this uncertainty. For his patience is great as his strength. Once, however, when dense clouds had lain between him and the earth for many days, so that he hardly knew any more whether he had not merely dreamed everything—the world and men and time—he called his right hand, which had so long been banished from his sight and hidden in small, unimportant works. It came willingly; for it believed that God wanted at last to forgive it. When God saw it there before him in its beauty, youth and strength, he was indeed inclined to forgiveness. But he remembered in time and commanded, without looking at it: 'You are to go down to earth. You are to take on the form you will see there among men, and to stand, naked, upon a mountain, so that I can observe you closely. As soon as you arrive below, go to a young woman and say to her, but very gently: I want to live. At first there will be a little darkness about you and then a great darkness, which is called childhood, and then you will be a man, and climb the mountain as I have commanded you. All this will of course last but a moment. Farewell.'

The right hand then took leave of the left, called it many gracious names—indeed, it has even been declared that it suddenly bowed down before it and said: 'Hail, Holy Ghost.' But here Saint Paul stepped up and smote off God's right hand; and an archangel caught it up and bore it away under his wide mantle. But God held the wound to with his left hand, so that his blood should not stream over the stars and thence fall down in sorrowful drops upon the earth. A short time after, God, watching attentively all that went on below, saw that certain men in iron garments were busying themselves about one mountain more than all others. And he expected to see his hand climb up there. But there came only a man in, as it seemed, a red cloak, who was dragging upwards some black swaying thing. At the same instant, God's left hand, lying over his open wound, began to grow restless, and suddenly, before God could prevent it, it left its place and rushed about madly among the stars, crying: 'Oh poor right hand, and I cannot help you!' Therewith it tugged hard at God's left arm, at the extremity of which it hung, trying to tear itself free. And the whole earth was red with God's blood, and it was impossible to see what was happening beneath it. At that time God had very nearly died. With a last effort he called his right hand back; it came pale and trembling and lay down in its place like a sick animal. And even the left hand, which already knew a good deal, since it had recognized the right down on the earth as it toiled up the mountain in a red cloak, could not learn from it what had further happened on that hill. It must have been something terrible. For God's right hand has not yet recovered from it, and suffers under its memories no less than under the ancient wrath of God, who has still not yet forgiven his hands."

My voice took a little rest. The stranger had covered his face with his hands. Thus everything stayed for a long time. Then the stranger said, in a voice I had long known: "And why have you told *me* this story?"

"Who else would have understood me? You come to me without rank, without office, without temporal honors, almost without a name. It was dark as you came in, yet I noticed in your features a resemblance—"

The stranger looked up, questioning.

"Yes," I answered his silent gaze, "I often think perhaps God's hand is again on its way . . ."

The children have heard this story, and evidently it was told them in such a way that they could understand everything; for they are very fond of this story.

Why God
Wants Poor People

⚜

THE FOREGOING story has spread so far and wide that the good schoolmaster goes about town looking very much pained. I can understand that. It is always bad for a teacher when the children suddenly know something which he has not told them. The teacher should, so to speak, be the only hole in the fence through which one can see into the orchard; if there are other holes too, the children will press around a different one every day and will soon tire of the view anyhow. I would not have drawn this comparison here, for perhaps not every teacher would agree to being a hole; but the schoolmaster of whom I speak, my neighbor, heard the comparison from me first and moreover considered it extremely apt. And even if somebody should think otherwise, the authority of my neighbor is decisive for me.

He stood before me, fidgeted constantly with his glasses, and said: "I don't know who told the children this story, but in any case it is not right to overload and strain their imagination with such extraordinary notions. The story in question is a kind of fairy-tale—"

"I happen to have heard it," I interrupted. (I was not lying, for since that evening it really had been repeated to me by the lady next door.)

"So," said the schoolmaster; that seemed to him easily explicable. "And what do you think of it?"

I hesitated, and he very quickly went on, too:

"In the first place, I think it wrong to treat religious, especially biblical, subjects in a free and arbitrary manner. At any rate, it has all been so expressed in the Catechism that it could not be better said . . ."

I was about to comment, but remembered just in time that the good schoolmaster had used "in the first place," so that now, according to the syntax and for the health of his sentence, there must follow a "then" and perhaps even an "and finally," ere I might permit myself to add something. And so it happened. As the schoolmaster has also delivered this very sentence, the faultless construction of which will delight every connoisseur, to others who would be no better able than I to forget it, I will here record only that which came, like the finale of some overture, after the beautiful preparatory words: "And finally."

"And finally . . . (letting pass the very fantastic conception) it seems to me the content hasn't even been sufficiently explored and considered from every angle. If I had time to write stories—"

"You miss something in this particular story?" I could not refrain from interrupting.

"Yes, I miss a good deal. From the literary-critical point of view, as it were. If I may speak to you as a colleague . . ."

I did not understand what he meant and said modestly: "You are too kind, but I have never done any teaching. . . ." Suddenly a thought struck me, I broke off, and he continued somewhat coolly:

"To take just one instance: it is not to be assumed that God (if one wants to go so far into the meaning of the story) that is, that God—I say—that God should have made no further attempt to see man as he is, I mean—"

Now I thought I should propitiate the good schoolmaster again. I made a little bow and began:

"Everybody knows that you have devoted yourself wholeheartedly (and, if one may say so, not without finding reciprocal affection) to a close study of the social question." The good schoolmaster smiled. "Well, then I may assume that what I now propose to tell you will not be altogether remote from your interest, especially as it enables me to link up with your last, very perspicacious remark."

He looked at me with astonishment. "You wouldn't mean that God . . ."

"Indeed," I confirmed, "God is just on the point of making a new attempt."

"Really!" the schoolmaster rebuked me. "And is that known to the authorities?"

"As to that, I can't tell you anything definite," said I regretfully. "I am not in touch with those circles; but if you nevertheless want to hear my little story . . . ?"

"You would be doing me a great favor." The schoolmaster took off his spectacles and carefully polished the lenses, while his naked eyes seemed to be ashamed.

I began:

"Once God was looking down into a great city. As his
eyes wearied of all the confusion (to which the networks
of electric wires contributed not a little) he decided to limit
his gaze for a while to a single tall apartment house, as this
was far less taxing. Simultaneously he remembered his old
wish to see a living man, and to this end his glances dove
into the windows of each storey in turn, from the lowest up.
The people on the first floor (a rich merchant and family)
were almost all clothes. Not only that all parts of their
bodies were covered with costly stuffs; the outlines of this
apparel were in many places so formed that one saw there
could no longer be a body underneath. On the second floor
it was not much better. The people who lived on the third
floor had distinctly fewer clothes on, but were so dirty that
God discerned only gray furrows, and in his goodness was
all ready to command that they should be fruitful. At last,
in a little slanting room under the roof, God found a man
in a shabby coat who was busy kneading clay. 'Oho, where
did you get that?' he cried. The man did not even take his
pipe from his mouth, growling: 'The devil knows where.
I wish I had become a cobbler. Here I sit and worry. . . .'
And ask what God might, the man was in a bad humor and
gave no more answer. Until one day he got a large letter
from the mayor of that town. Then, unasked, he told God
everything. He had had no commission for so long. Now,
suddenly, he was to make a statue for the public park, and
it was to be called: Truth. The sculptor worked day and
night in a distant studio, and to God came various old
memories as he saw this. Had he not still been angry with
his hands, he too would surely have begun to make some-

thing again. But as the day came when the statue that was called Truth was to be carried out to its place in the gardens, where God too could have seen it in its perfection, a great to-do arose, for a commission of city fathers, schoolmasters and other influential personalities had demanded that the figure should first be partially clothed, before the public viewed it. God did not understand why, so loudly did the sculptor swear. City fathers, schoolmasters and the rest it was, who brought him to this sin, and God will surely— But you are coughing terribly!"

"It will pass," said my schoolmaster in a perfectly clear voice.

"Well, I have but a little more to tell. God let go the apartment house and the public park and intended to withdraw his gaze altogether, as one pulls a fishing-rod out of water, with a swing, to see if anything has bitten. This time something actually hung there. A little tiny house with several people in it, who all had very little on, for they were very poor. 'That's it, then—' thought God, 'people have to be poor. These, I believe, are already very poor, but I will make them so poor that they haven't even a shirt to put on.' This God undertook to do."

Here I made a full stop in my talk, to indicate that I had come to the end. The good schoolmaster was not satisfied with that; he found this story just as little finished and rounded off as the preceding.

"Yes,"—I excused myself—"a poet ought to get hold of that story and invent some sort of fantastical ending, for in fact it has no end yet."

"How so?" queried the good schoolmaster and looked

at me expectantly.

"But, dear Mister Schoolmaster," I reminded him, "how forgetful you are! Are you not yourself a director of our local charities . . . ?"

"Yes, I have been for some ten years, but—?"

"That's just it. You and your society have been preventing God for the longest time from attaining his object. You clothe the people—"

"Oh, don't mention it," said the schoolmaster modestly, "that is simply charity, love of one's neighbor. It is of course pleasing to God in the highest degree."

"Ah, and of that they are quite convinced in authoritative circles?" I asked guilelessly.

"Naturally we are. In my capacity as member of the board of directors of the local charities not a little praise has come to my ears. I'll tell you in confidence that when the next promotions take place my activities in this field— you understand?" The good schoolmaster blushed bashfully.

"Accept my very best wishes," I responded. We shook hands, and the worthy man went his way with such proud, measured steps that I am sure he must have been late for school.

As I learned later, a part of this story (insofar as it is suitable for them) became known to the children after all. Would the good schoolmaster have composed an ending for it?

How Treason Came to Russia

I HAVE another friend here in the neighborhood. This is a fair-haired, lame man who has his chair, summer and winter, close by the window. He can look very young; in his listening face there is often something boyish. But there are also days on which he ages, when the minutes pass over him like years, and suddenly he is an old man, whose dim eyes have already almost let go of life. We have known each other long. At first we always looked at each other, later we smiled involuntarily, for a whole year we bowed, and since God knows when we have been telling each other one thing and another, indiscriminately, just as it happens.

"Good morning," he called as I came by, his window still being open, out into the rich and quiet autumn. "I have not seen you for a long time."

"Good morning, Ewald—" I stepped up to his window as I always did in passing. "I was away."

"Where have you been?" he asked with impatient eyes.

"To Russia."

"Oh, so far—" he leaned back, and then: "What kind

of a country is it, Russia? Very large, isn't it?"

"Yes," said I, "it is large and besides—"

"Was that a stupid question?" smiled Ewald, and he blushed.

"No, Ewald, on the contrary. Your asking, what kind of country is it? makes various things clear to me. For instance, how Russia is bounded."

"On the East?" my friend threw in.

I reflected: "No."

"On the North?" inquired the lame man.

"You see,"—I had an inspiration—"the reading of maps has spoiled people. There, everything is flat and level, and when they have noted the four points of the compass, they think that's all. But a country is no map. It has mountains and precipices. It must touch against something both above and below."

"Hm—" my friend considered. "You are right. On what could Russia border in those two directions?" Suddenly the invalid looked like a boy.

"You've got it!" I exclaimed.

"Perhaps on God?"

"Yes," I confirmed, "on God."

"So—," my friend nodded, in full understanding. Only then did certain doubts come to him. "But is God a country?"

"I don't think so," I replied, "but in primitive languages many things have the same name. There is probably a kingdom called God, and he who reigns over it is also called God. Simple peoples cannot always distinguish their country from their king; both are great and good, terrible and great."

"I understand," the man at the window said slowly. "And does one notice this proximity in Russia?"

"One notices it all the time. The influence of God is very powerful. However much one may bring from Europe, all Western things are stones as soon as they are over the frontier. Now and again precious stones, but only for the rich, the so-called 'educated classes,' while from beyond, from the other kingdom, comes the bread on which the people live."

"And which they probably have in abundance?"

I hesitated: "No, that is not the case. Certain circumstances make the imports from God difficult—" I tried to divert him from this thought. "But they have adopted many of the customs of that broad neighbor country. All the ceremony, for instance. You speak to the Tsar as you would to God."

"Oh, so you don't say 'Your Majesty'?"

"No, you call them both 'Little Father.' "

"And you kneel to them both as well?"

"You throw yourself down before both of them, touch the earth with your forehead, and weep and say: 'I am a sinner, forgive me, Little Father.' We, seeing that, call it slavery and most unworthy. I think differently about it. What does kneeling signify? It is meant to declare: I am full of reverence. But you can do that well enough by uncovering your head, say we. Well, yes—raising your hat, bowing —they are also in a way expressions of it, abbreviations that have come about in those countries where there was not so much room that everybody could throw themselves on the ground. But abbreviations we soon use mechanically, no longer aware of their meaning. That is why it is good, where there is still room and time to do so, to write the gesture out in full, the whole beautiful and weighty word: reverence."

"Yes, if I could, I too would kneel down—"mused the lame man.

"But in Russia," I continued after a pause, "many other things too come from God. One feels that everything new is introduced by him, every garment, every dish, every virtue and even every sin must first have his sanction before it comes into use." The sick man looked at me almost frightened. "It is only a fairy-tale I refer to," I hastened to reassure him, "a so-called *bylina,* something that has been, as we would say. I will briefly tell you the substance of it. The title is: 'How Treason Came to Russia.'" I leaned against the window and the lame man closed his eyes, as he liked to do when a story was about to begin.

"The terrible Tsar Ivan wanted to lay tribute upon the neighboring princes and threatened them with a great war if they would not send gold to Moscow, the white city. The princes, after due deliberation, spoke as one man: 'We give you three riddles to solve. Come, on the day we appoint, to the East, to the white stone, where we shall be gathered, and tell us the three answers. If they are correct, we will at once give you the twelve barrels of gold that you demand of us.' At first Tsar Ivan Vassilievitch reflected, but the many bells of his white city of Moscow disturbed him. So he called his wise men and councilors before him, and each one who could not answer the riddles he caused to be led out to the great red square, where the church of Vassily the Naked was just being built, and simply beheaded. Thus occupied, time passed so quickly for him that he suddenly found himself on his way to the East, to the white stone by which the princes waited. To none of the three questions had he any answer, but the ride was long and there was still always the possibility of meeting a wise man; for at that time many wise men were in flight, as all kings had the habit of ordering their heads cut off if they did not seem to them wise enough. Now the Tsar did not happen to run across any such person, but one morning he saw an old bearded peasant who was building at a church. He had already got as far as the frame-work of the roof and was laying on the small laths. It seemed very odd that the old peasant should climb down from the church over and over again in order to fetch one by one the narrow laths which were piled below, instead of taking a lot at a time in his long caftan. In this way he had to climb up and down continually, and there seemed no prospect of his ever getting all those hundreds of laths into place. So the Tsar grew impatient: 'Idiot,' he cried (that is how one usually addresses the peasants in Russia), 'you ought to load yourself up well with your wood and then crawl up on the roof; that would be much simpler.'

The peasant, who at the moment was on the ground, stood still, shielded his eyes with his hand and replied: 'That you must leave to me, Tsar Ivan Vassilievitch; every man knows his own craft best; nevertheless, as you happen to be riding by, I will tell you the answer to the three riddles, which you will have to know when you get to the white stone in the East, not at all far from here.' And he urgently impressed the three answers in turn upon the Tsar's mind. The Tsar could hardly manage to thank him for astonishment. 'What shall I give you in reward?' he asked at last. 'Nothing,' said the peasant, fetched another lath and started up the ladder. 'Stop,' commanded the Tsar, 'this will never do. You must wish for something.' 'Well, Little Father, since you so command, give me one of the twelve barrels of gold you will get from the princes of the East.' 'Good,' the Tsar nodded, 'I will give you a barrel of gold.' Then he rode off quickly, lest he forget the answers again.

Later, when the Tsar had returned from the East with the twelve barrels of gold, he shut himself up in Moscow, in his palace, in the heart of the five-gated Kremlin, and he emptied one barrel after the other on the shining tiles of the hall, so that a veritable mountain of gold grew up that cast a great black shadow on the floor. In his forgetfulness the Tsar had emptied the twelfth cask too. He wanted to fill it up again, but it grieved him to have to take away so much gold from the glorious pile. In the night he went down into the courtyard, scooped fine sand into the barrel until it was three-quarters full, crept softly back into his palace, laid gold over the sand, and next morning sent the cask by messenger to that part of the broad land of Russia where the old peasant was building his church.

As he saw the messenger approaching, the peasant came down from the roof, which was still far from finished, and called out: 'You need come no nearer, my friend. Go back, with your barrel which is three-quarters full of sand

and contains but one scant quarter of gold; I do not need it. Tell your master that up to now there has been no treason in Russia. And it is his own fault, should he notice that he cannot rely on any man; for he has now shown the way of betrayal, and from century to century his example will find throughout Russia many imitators. I do not need the gold, I can live without gold; I did not expect gold from him, but truth and righteousness. But he has deceived me. Say that to your master, the terrible Tsar Ivan Vassilievitch, who sits in his white city of Moscow with his evil conscience and in a golden dress.'

After riding a while, the messenger looked back once more: the peasant and his church had vanished. And the piled laths no longer lay there; it was all empty, flat land. At that the man tore back in terror to Moscow, stood breathless before the Tsar and told him somewhat incoherently what had happened, and how the supposed peasant was no other than God himself."

"Could he have been right?" my friend asked softly when the last words of my story had died away.

"Perhaps—" I replied, "though, you know, the people are—superstitious. . . . But I must go now, Ewald."

"Too bad," said the lame man heartily. "Won't you tell me another story soon?"

"Gladly—but under one condition." I stepped to the window once more.

"Namely?" asked Ewald in surprise.

"You must, when you have a chance, repeat them all to the children in the neighborhood," I begged.

"Oh, the children come to me so seldom now."

45

I consoled him: "They'll come all right. Evidently you have not felt like telling them anything of late, and perhaps you had nothing to tell, or too much. But if some one knows a real story, do you believe that can remain a secret? Never fear, it gets told around, especially among the children! Good-bye." With that I left him.

And the children heard the story on the self-same day.

How Old Timofei
Died Singing

≫≪

WHAT A pleasure it is to tell stories to a la
Healthy people are so changeable; they look at ʁ
from this, now from that angle, and, when yoʳ
walking along with them on your right for ʳ
may suddenly answer you from your left, siʳ
occurs to them that that is more polite and shᵤ
refined upbringing. With a lame man one has not uₓ
fear. His immobility makes him resemble things, with which
indeed he fosters many intimacies; makes him, so to speak,
a thing far superior to other things, a thing that listens not
only with its silence but also with its rare, quiet words and
with its gentle, reverent feelings.

I like best telling stories to my friend Ewald. And I
was very glad when from his daily window he called to me:
"I must ask you something."

Quickly I went up and greeted him.

"Where did you get the story you told me last time?"
he begged me then. "Out of a book?"

"Yes," I answered sadly, "the historians have kept it
buried there, since it died; that is not so very long ago. Only

a hundred years since, it lived—quite carelessly, for sure—on many lips. But the words that people use now, those heavy words one cannot sing, were its enemies and took from it one mouth after another, so that in the end it lived, most withdrawn and impoverished, on one pair of dry lips, as on a miserable widow's portion. And there it died, leaving no heirs, and was, as I have already said, buried with all honors in a book where others of its family already lay."

"And it was very old when it died?" asked my friend, entering into the conceit.

"Four to five hundred years," I informed him truthfully; "some of its relations attained an even greater age."

"How, without ever coming to rest in a book?" Ewald wondered.

I explained: "So far as I know, they were traveling from mouth to mouth all the time."

"And did they never sleep?"

"Oh, yes, rising from the singer's lips, they might stay now and then in some heart, where it was warm and dark."

"But were people so quiet that songs could sleep in their hearts?" Ewald seemed to me thoroughly incredulous.

"They must have been. It is said that they spoke less, danced dances of slowly growing intensity that had something soothing in their sway, and above all, they did not laugh loudly, as one not infrequently hears them do to-day, despite our general high state of culture."

Ewald was on the point of asking another question, but he suppressed it and smiled. "I ask and ask—but perhaps you are about to tell me a story?" He looked at me expectantly.

"A story? I don't know. I only wanted to say that these songs were the heritage of certain families. One had taken it over and one passed it on, not quite untouched, with traces of daily use yet still undamaged, like an old bible that is handed down from father to son. A disinherited man differed from his brothers who had come into their rights in that he could not sing, or at least knew only a small part of the songs of his father and grandfather, and lost with the other songs that great piece of experience which all these *bylini* and *skaski* represent to the people.

Thus Yegor Timofeievitch, for example, had married against the will of his father, old Timofei, a beautiful young wife and had gone with her to Kiev, to the holy city, beside which the graves of the greatest martyrs of the Holy Orthodox Church are gathered. Father Timofei, who counted as the most adept singer within ten days' journey, cursed his son and told his neighbors he was often convinced that he had never had any such son at all. Nevertheless he grew dumb in rancor and sorrow. And he sent away all the young people who came crowding into his hut in order to become the heritors of the many songs that were locked up in the old man as in a dust-covered violin. 'Father, our little father, give us just one song or another. See, we will carry it into the villages, and you shall hear it in every farmyard as soon as evening comes and the cattle in the stables have quieted down.'

The old man, who sat continually on the stove, shook his head all day long. He no longer heard well, and as he never knew whether one of the lads who always hung listening around his house now, had not just asked for a song again, he would sign with his white head tremulously: No, no, no, till he fell asleep and even then a while—in sleep. He would gladly have done as the young men asked; he himself was sorry that his dumb, dead dust was to lie upon these songs, perhaps quite soon now. But had he tried to teach one of them something, he would surely have had to remember his own Yegorushka, and then—who knows what might have happened then? For only because in general he kept silence had no one seen him weep. It was there, the sobbing, behind every word, and he always had to close his mouth very quickly and carefully, lest sometime it should come out too.

Old Timofei had begun very early to teach his only son Yegor certain songs, and as a boy of fifteen Yegor could already sing more, and more correctly, than all the grown-up youths in the village and the neighborhood. At the same time the old man, mostly of a holiday when he was somewhat drunk, would say to the lad: 'Yegorushka, my little dove, I have already taught you to sing many songs, many bylini and also the legends of the Saints, one for every day almost. But as you know, I am the most accomplished singer of the whole government, and my father knew, so to speak, all the songs of the whole of Russia, and also Tatar stories as well. You are still very young, and so I have not yet told you the most beautiful bylini, in which the words are like ikons and not at all to be compared with ordinary words, and you have not yet learned to sing those melodies that no man ever, were he Cossack or peasant, has been able to listen to without weeping.'

This Timofei repeated to his son every Sunday and on

all the many holidays of the Russian year—that is, quite often. Until Yegor, after a violent scene with the old man, disappeared, simultaneously with the beautiful Ustionka, the daughter of a poor peasant.

In the third year after this event, Timofei fell ill, at the very time when one of those many pilgrimages that are always on their way from all parts of the vast empire to Kiev, was about to start. His neighbor Ossip came to see the sick man: 'I am going with the pilgrims, Timofei Ivanitch, permit me to embrace you before I go.' Ossip was no particular friend of the old man, but now that he was starting on this long journey, he found it absolutely necessary to take leave of him as of a father. 'I have sometimes offended you,' he sobbed, 'forgive me, my little heart, it happened in drunkenness, and then one can't help it, as you know. Now I will pray for you and light a candle for you. Farewell, Timofei Ivanitch, my little father, perhaps you will get well again, if God wills it; then you will sing for us once more. Ah, yes, it is a long time since you have sung. What songs those were! The one about Diuk Stepanovitch, for instance, do you think I have forgotten it? How stupid you are! I still know it perfectly. Of course, not like you—*you* simply knew how to sing it, one must admit. God has given you *that*, to another he gives something *else*. To me, for instance . . .'

The old man, who was lying on the stove, turned round with a groan and made a movement as though he would say something. It sounded, very softly, like Yegor's name. Perhaps he wanted to send him a message. But when Ossip, from the door, asked: 'Did you say something, Timofei Ivanitch?' he lay quite still again and only shook his white head gently. All the same, God knows how it happened, hardly a year after Ossip had gone away, Yegor quite unexpectedly returned. The aged man did not recognize him at once, for it was dark in the hut, and the old eyes were reluctant to take in a new, unfamiliar figure. But when Timofei heard the stranger's voice, he started and jumped down from the stove on his rickety old legs. Yegor caught him, and they clasped each other in their arms. Timofei wept. The young man asked over and over: 'Have you been ill a long time, Father?' When the old man had regained a little composure, he crept back on his stove and inquired in a changed, a severe tone: 'And your wife?'

A pause. Yegor spat. 'I have sent her away, you know, with the child.' He was silent a while. 'One day Ossip comes to see me. "Ossip Nikiforovitch?" say I. "Yes," he answers, "it is I. Your father is sick, Yegor. He can no longer sing. It is all silent now in the village, as though it had no soul any more, our village. Nothing knocks, nothing stirs, no one weeps any more, and there's no real reason to laugh either." I think it over. What's to be done? So I call my wife. "Ustionka"—say I—"I must go home, no one else is singing there now, it is my turn. Father is sick." "Good," says Ustionka. "But I cannot take you with me," I explain, "Father, you know, won't have you. And probably I shall not come back to you either, once I am there again and singing." Ustionka understands me. "Well, God be with you. There are many pilgrims here now, there'll be alms aplenty. God will help, Yegor." And so I went away. And now, Father, tell me all your songs.'

The rumor spread that Yegor had come back and that old Timofei was singing again. But that autumn the wind went so violently through the village that none of those who passed by could tell for sure whether there really was singing in Timofei's house or not. And the door was not opened to any one who knocked. The two wanted to be alone. Yegor sat on the edge of the stove on which his father lay, now and then bringing his ear close to the old man's lips, for he was indeed singing. His aged voice bore, somewhat bent and trembling, all his most beautiful songs to Yegor, and Yegor would sometimes sway his head or swing his hanging legs, quite as though he were already singing himself. This went on for many days. Timofei kept finding some still more beautiful song in his memory; often, at night, he would wake his son and while he gestured uncertainly with his withered, twitching hands, he would sing one little song and then another and yet another—till the lazy morning began to stir. Soon after singing the most beautiful he died. He had often bitterly complained in his last days that he still carried a vast quantity of songs within him and had no time left to impart them to his son. He lay there with furrowed brow, in intense and fearful recollection, and his lips trembled with expectancy. From time to time he would sit upright, sway his head to and fro for a while, move his lips—and at length some faint little song would come forth; but now for the most part, he kept singing the same verses about Diuk Stepanovitch, which he particularly loved, and his son had to appear astonished and pretend he was hearing them for the first time, in order not to anger him.

After old Timofei Ivanitch had died, the house, in which his son now lived alone, remained shut up for a time. Then, in the following spring, Yegor Timofeievitch, who now had quite a long beard, stepped out of his door, and began to walk about the village and sing. Later he visited the neighboring villages too, and the peasants began to tell each other that Yegor had become at least as accomplished a singer as his father Timofei; for he knew a great number of grave and heroic songs and all those melodies to which no man, were he Cossack or peasant, could listen without weeping. Besides, his voice is supposed to have had such a soft and sorrowful tone as had never been heard from any other singer. And this quality always appeared, quite unexpectedly, in the refrain, which was therefore particularly moving in effect. So at least I have heard tell."

"Then he did not learn that tone from his father?" asked my friend Ewald after a while.

"No," I answered, "it is not known how he came by it."

I had already stepped away from the window, but the lame man moved again and called after me:

"Perhaps he was thinking of his wife and his child. Tell me, did he never send for them, his father being dead?"

"No, I don't think so. At least he was alone later on when he died."

The Song of Justice

∾

THE NEXT time I passed Ewald's window, he waved to me and smiled. "Did you promise the children something definite?"

"How so?" I asked in surprise.

"Well, when I had told them the story of Yegor, they complained that God did not come into it."

I was startled. "What, a story without God? But how is that possible?" Then I remembered: "Indeed, it is true; that story, as I now think it over, says nothing about God. I can't understand how that could happen; had some one asked me for a story, I believe I should have thought all my life, in vain . . ."

My friend smiled at this agitation. "You must not take it to heart," he interrupted with a certain kindliness. "I imagine one can never tell whether God is in a story before one has finished it completely. For if only two words of the telling are still missing—indeed, if nothing but the pause after the last word is still outstanding, he may yet come." I nodded, and the lame man went on in a different tone: "Don't you know something more about those Russian singers?"

I demurred. "Yes, but should we not rather talk about

God, Ewald?"

He shook his head. "I want so much to hear more about those singular men. I don't know how it happens, I always imagine if one of them were to come in here—" and he turned his head towards the room, in the direction of the door. Then his eyes came back to me quickly and not without embarrassment. "But of course that would hardly be possible," he amended hastily.

"Why should it not be possible, Ewald? Many things might come to you that are not vouchsafed to people who can use their legs, because they pass so much by and run away from so many things. God has destined you, Ewald, to be a calm point amidst all the hurry. Don't you feel how everything moves around you? Other people are always chasing after their days, and when they do catch up with one, they are so out of breath that they cannot talk with it at all. But you, my friend, simply sit at your window and wait; and to those who wait something always happens. You have a quite particular destiny. Just think, even the Iberian Madonna in Moscow must leave her little shrine and she drives in a black coach with four horses to those who are celebrating something, be it a christening or a death. But to you *everything* must come—"

"Yes," said Ewald with a remote simle, "I cannot even go to meet Death. Many people find him as they go their ways. He fights shy of entering their houses, and calls them away to foreign lands, to war, up onto a high tower, onto a swaying bridge, into some bewilderment or into madness. Most of them at least fetch him from somewhere outside and then carry him home on their shoulders all unwittingly.

For Death is lazy; if people were not always disturbing him, who knows, he might even fall asleep." The sick man pondered a while, and then continued with a certain pride:

"But to me he will have to come when he wants me. Here into my sunny little room, where the flowers keep fresh so long, over this old carpet, past this cupboard, between the table and the foot of the bed (it's not so easy to squeeze through), right here to my dear old comfortable chair, which will then probably die with me because it has, so to speak, lived with me. And he will have to do all this in the usual way, like any visitor, without noise, without knocking anything over, without doing anything out of the ordinary. That is what brings my room extraordinarily close to me. It will all be acted out on this narrow stage, and that is why this last episode will not differ so very much from all the other events that have taken place here and are yet to come. Even when I was a child, it always seemed strange to me that people should speak so differently of Death from the way they speak of other incidents, and that only because nobody divulges to us what happens to him afterwards. But how then is a dead man to be distinguished from a person who turns serious, renounces time and locks himself in, in order to reflect quietly about something the solution of which has long been worrying him? Among people one can't even remember the Lord's Prayer; how then remember some other more mysterious context that may consist not of words, but of events? One must go apart into some inaccessible stillness; and perhaps the dead are such as have withdrawn in order to reflect upon life."

There ensued a brief silence, to which I put an end

with the following words: "That makes me think of a certain young girl. One might say that she spent the first seventeen years of her happy life entirely in *looking*. Her eyes were so large and so self-reliant that they themselves consumed all they received, and the life in the young creature's whole body went on independently of them, nourished by its own smooth inner stirrings. At the end of that time, however, some too-violent event disturbed this double life whose courses scarcely touched, the eyes seemed to break through, back into her inner being, and the whole weight of the outside fell through them into her dark heart, and each new day plunged so heavily into that deep, steepdown gaze that it burst like a glass in her slender breast. Then the young girl grew pale, began to sicken, to be much alone, to meditate, and in the end herself sought that stillness in which thoughts are probably no longer disturbed."

"How did she die?" asked my friend softly, his voice slightly husky.

"She was drowned. In a deep, still pool, and on the surface of it many circles formed, slowly widening and growing away under the white waterlilies, so that all those bathing blossoms stirred."

"Is that a story too?" asked Ewald, to keep the silence behind my words from taking over.

"No," I answered, "it is a feeling, an emotion."

"But couldn't one convey it to the children too—that emotion?"

I pondered. "Perhaps—"

"And how?"

"By another story." And I began:

"It was at the time when they were fighting for freedom in southern Russia."

"Forgive me," interrupted Ewald, "how am I to understand that? Did the people want to get rid of the Tsar? That wouldn't correspond with my idea of Russia, and would be inconsistent with what you have told me before. If that is the case, I should prefer not to hear your story. For I love the picture I have made for myself of things there, and want to keep it unspoiled."

That made me smile and I reassured him. "The Polish Pans (I should have said that in the beginning) were masters in southern Russia and in those silent, solitary steppes that are known as the Ukraine. They were hard masters. Their tyranny and the cupidity of the Jews, who even held the keys of the churches and would only let the true believers have them for money, had made the young people about Kiev and all the way up the Dnieper weary and thoughtful. The city itself, Kiev, the holy, the place where Russia first gave account of herself with four hundred church domes, sank always more into itself and consumed itself in fires as if in sudden, lunatic thoughts, behind which the night only grows more and more immense.

The people of the steppe did not rightly know what was happening. But, seized with singular unrest, the old men would leave their huts at night and gaze silently into the high, eternally windless heavens, and by day one could see figures appear on the ridges of the kurgans and stand waiting, silhouetted against the flat distance. These kurgans are burial-mounds of bygone generations and spread across the entire plain like a frozen, sleeping succession of waves. And in this country, where graves are the mountains, men are the abysses. Deep, dark, silent are these people, and their words are but weak, swaying bridges over their real being. —Sometimes dark birds fly up from the kurgans. Sometimes wild songs drop down into these crepuscular people and vanish deep inside them, while the birds are lost in the sky. In all directions, everything seems limitless. Even the houses are no protection against this immeasurableness; their little windows are full of it. Only in the darkening corners of the rooms the old ikons stand, like milestones of God, and the glint of a tiny light runs over their frames like a lost child through the starry night. These ikons are the only hold, the only reliable sign on the way, and no house can endure without them. More are needed all the time; when one goes to pieces with age and worms, or when somebody marries and builds himself a hut, or when a person like old Abraham, for instance, dies with the wish to take Saint Nicholas, the worker of miracles, with him in his folded hands, probably in order to compare the saints in heaven with the image and to recognize this especially honored one before all others.

So it comes that Peter Akimovitch, properly a shoe-maker by profession, also paints ikons. When he tires of the one labor, he changes, after he has crossed himself three times, to the other, and over his sewing and hammering, as well as his painting, the same piety holds sway. He is already an old man now, but quite robust. His back, which he bends over the boots, he straightens up again before the pictures, and thus he has preserved a good posture and a certain equilibrium in shoulders and loins. The greater part of his life he has spent all alone, never mingling in the excitement which came of his wife Akulina bearing him children and of these dying or getting married. Not till his seventieth year had Peter got into touch with those who had been dwelling in his house and whom he now for the first time looked upon as really present. These were: Akulina, his wife, a quiet, humble person, who had spent herself almost wholly in her children; an ageing, ugly daughter, and Alyosha, a son, who, born disproportionately late in his father's life, was only seventeen. This son Peter wanted to train in painting; for he realized that he alone would not be able to cope much longer with all the orders. But he soon abandoned the lessons. Alyosha had painted the most holy Virgin, but had so little achieved the austere and correct image he was copying, that his handiwork looked like a portrait of Mariana, the daughter of Golokopytenko the Cossack—that is, like something thoroughly sinful—and old Peter hastened, after crossing himself many times, to paint over the offended panel with a Saint Dmitri, whom for some unknown reason he set above all other saints.

Nor did Alyosha ever again try to begin a picture. When his father had not ordered him to gild a halo, he was usually out on the steppe, no one knew where. Nobody kept him at home. His mother wondered about him and was shy of speaking to him, as though he were a stranger or an official. His sister had always beaten him when he was a child, and now that Alyosha had grown up she began to despise him because *he* did not beat *her*. Neither was there anybody in the village who bothered about the boy. Mariana, the Cossack's daughter, had laughed at him when he told her he wanted to marry her, and thereafter Alyosha had not asked the other girls if they would accept him as a bridegroom. Nobody had wanted to take him into the Setch, to the Zaporozhian Cossacks, because they all thought him too weakly and perhaps also a little young yet. Once he had run away to the nearest monastery, but the monks did not take him in—and so only the plain remained to him, the broad, billowing plain. A hunter had once given him an old gun, loaded with God knows what. Alyosha always dragged it about with him, but never fired it, first, because he wanted to save the bullet, and then, because he did not know what to shoot.

One warm quiet evening at the beginning of summer they all sat together at the rough-hewn table, on which stood a dish of meal. Peter ate, and the others watched him and waited for what he should leave. Suddenly the old man stopped with his spoon in mid-air and stretched his broad wrinkled head into the streak of light that came from the doorway and ran straight across the table into the dusk beyond. They all listened. Outside, along the walls of the hut, there was a sound as though some night-bird were gently brushing against the beams with its wings; but the sun had scarcely set, and anyway, nocturnal birds rarely ventured into the village. And then again it seemed as though some other large animal were tapping its way round the house, and as though its groping tread were perceptible from all the walls at once. Aloysha rose quietly from his bench. At the same moment the door was darkened by something high, black; it pushed the whole evening aside, brought night into the hut, and could only move forward unsteadily in its great bulk. 'Ostap!' said the ugly girl in her harsh voice. And now they all recognized him. It was one of the blind kobzars, an old man who wandered through the villages with a twelve-stringed bandura and sang of the great fame of the Cossacks, of their braveness and loyalty, of their hetmans Kirdiaga, Kukubenko, Bulba, and other heroes, so that everyone loved to listen. Ostap bowed three times in the direction in which he guessed the holy image to be (and it was the Znamenskaya to whom he thus instinctively turned), sat down near the stove and asked in a low voice: 'In whose house might I be?'

'In ours, little father, in the house of Peter Akimovitch, the shoemaker,' answered Peter affably. He was a lover of song and glad of this unexpected visit.

'Ah, Peter Akimovitch, the one who paints ikons,' said the blind man, returning the courtesy. Then there was silence. In the long six strings of the bandura a sound began, grew and came back brittle and as if exhausted from the six short strings, and this effect kept recurring in ever quickening measure, so that finally one had to close one's eyes for fear of seeing the tone hurtle down from some height to which the melody had mounted in such a delirious onrush; then the instrument broke off and gave way to the fine, strong voice of the kobzar, which soon filled the whole house and called the people out of the neighboring huts too, who gathered before the door and underneath the windows. But not of heroes did the song tell this time. The fame of Bulba and Ostranitza and Nalivaiko seemed already secure. Firm for all time seemed the faith of the Cossacks. Nor of their deeds did the song tell that day. The spirit of the dance seemed to sleep deeper in all who heard; for no one moved a leg or raised a hand. Like Ostap's head, so were the other heads bowed, growing heavy with the sorrowful song:

'There is no Justice more in the world. Justice, who can find her? There is no Justice more in the world: for all Justice has become subject to the laws of Injustice.

'To-day Justice lies wretched in chains. And Wrong laughs at her, we have seen it, and sits with the Pans in their golden seats and sits in the golden hall with the Pans.

'Justice lies on the threshold, imploring; Wrong, which is Evil, is the guest of the Pans, who beckon it laughing into their palace and they pour Wrong a cup full with mead.

'Oh, Justice, little mother, little mother mine, with a wing that is like to the eagle's, there may yet come a man who wants to be just, to be just; then help him God, He alone can, and makes light the days of the just.'

And only with effort were the heads lifted and on all brows stood silence; this they too saw who would have spoken. And after a short, solemn pause, the playing on the bandura began again, this time already better understood by the ever growing crowd. Three times Ostap sang his Song of Justice. And each time it was a different song. If the first time it was a lament, upon repetition it seemed a reproach, and finally, when at the third time the kobzar with high-thrown head shouted it like a chain of curt commands, a wild fury broke from the quivering words and took possession of the listeners and carried them all away in a spreading and yet anxious enthusiasm.

'Where do the men meet?' asked a young peasant, as the singer arose. The old man, who was informed of all the movements of the Cossacks, named a place near by. The men dispersed rapidly, sharp calls were heard, the stir of arms, and women wept in the doorways. An hour later a company of peasants, armed, marched out of the village towards Chernigov.

Peter had offered the kobzar a glass of cider in the hope of learning more from him. The old man sat and drank, but gave only brief replies to the shoemaker's many questions. Then he thanked his host and went. Alyosha led the blind man over the threshold. When they were out in the night and alone, Alyosha asked, beseeching: 'And may everybody go to the war?'

'Everybody,' said the old man and vanished with quickened stride, as though the night would lend him vision.

When all were asleep, Alyosha rose from the stove, where he had been lying in his clothes, took his gun and went forth. Outside, he felt himself suddenly embraced and gently kissed on the hair. Next moment he recognized Akulina in the moonlight, tripping hastily towards the house. 'Mother?!' he exclaimed, and a strange feeling came over him. He hesitated a while. A door opened and closed somewhere, and a dog howled near by. Then Alyosha slung his gun over his shoulder and strode stoutly away, for he thought to catch up with the men before morning.

In the house they all acted as though they did not notice Alyosha's absence. Only, when they sat down to table once more and Peter became aware of the empty place, he got up again, went into the corner and lit a candle before the Znamenskaya. A very thin candle. The ugly girl shrugged her shoulders.

Meanwhile, Ostap, the blind old man, was already on

his way through the next village, beginning sadly and with gently lamenting voice the Song of Justice." . . .

The lame man waited yet a while. Then he looked at me in surprise. "Well, why don't you finish? It is the same as in the story about treason. That old man was God."

"Oh, and I didn't know!" said I, tingling at the thought.

A Scene from
the Ghetto of Venice

☙❧

HERR BAUM, householder, Chairman of the Borough
Council, Honorary Chief of the Volunteer Fire Brigade,
and various other things as well—or, to put it briefly, Herr
Baum—must have overhead one of my conversations with
Ewald. No wonder; to him belongs the house on the
ground floor of which my friend lives. Herr Baum and I
have known each other by sight for a long time. But the
other day, the chairman of the Borough Council stops,
raises his hat a little, so that a small bird could have flown
out in the event that one had been caught under it, smiles
politely and opens our acquaintance with the words:
"You travel sometimes?"
"Oh, yes—" I answered, rather vaguely, "I very well
may."
Then he went on confidentially: "I believe we are the
only two here who have been in Italy."
"Indeed—" I made an effort to be a little more atten-
tive, "well, then of course it is urgently necessary that we
should talk together."
Herr Baum laughed. "Italy, to be sure—that really is

something. I am always telling my children—. Take Venice, for example!

I stopped. "You still remember Venice?"

"But, I put it to you," he groaned, for he was rather too stout to become indignant without exertion, "how could I fail to? When you've once seen it—that Piazzetta—don't you agree?"

"Yes," I answered, "I remember with particular pleasure the ride through the Canal, that soft soundless gliding along the borders of things past."

"The Palazzo Franchetti!" he exclaimed.

"The Cà d'Oro—" I rejoined.

"The Fishmarket—"

"The Palazzo Vendramin—"

"Where Richard Wagner—" he, as a German of culture, hastily added.

I nodded. "The Ponte, you remember?"

He smiled, well oriented. "Of course, and the Museum, not to forget the Academy, where a Titian . . ."

Thus Herr Baum had put himself through a kind of examination, which was rather taxing. I undertook to compensate him with a story. And began forthwith:

"When you pass along under the Ponte di Rialto, skirting the Fondaco de' Turchi and the Fishmarket, and tell your gondolier 'to the right!' he will look surprised and may even ask 'Dove?' But you insist on going to the right, you leave the gondola in one of the dirty little canals, bargain with the gondolier, tell him what you think of him, and walk away through narrow alleys and black, smoke-darkened archways, out onto an empty, open square. All this for the simple reason that my story takes place there."

Herr Baum diffidently touched my arm. "Pardon me, what story?" His small eyes darted hither and thither in some anxiety.

I reassured him: "Oh, just a little story, my dear sir, nothing remarkable at all. I cannot even tell you when it happened. Perhaps under Doge Alvise Mocenigo IV, but it may also have been somewhat earlier or somewhat later. Carpaccio's pictures, if you happen to have seen some of them, look as though they were painted on purple velvet, everywhere something warm, sylvan, as it were, breaks through, and around the subdued lights in there listening shadows crowd. Giorgione painted on dull, ageing gold, Titian on black satin, but at the time of which I speak, light pictures were in favor, done on a ground of white silk, and the name that was toyed with, that lovely lips threw out into the sunlight and charming ears caught up as it fell quivering down—that name is Gian Battista Tiepolo.

But all this does not come into my story. Only the real Venice is concerned, the city of palaces, of adventures, of masques and pale nights on the lagoon, which carry like no other nights the sound of clandestine romances.—In the bit of Venice of which I shall tell, there are only poor ordinary sounds, the days pass monotonously over it, as though they were but a single day, and the songs one hears there are swelling plaints that do not mount upward but settle like curling smoke over the alleys. As soon as twilight comes, much furtive humanity mills about the streets, countless children have their homes upon the squares and in the narrow cold doorways and play with chips and leavings of varicolored glassy flux, the same from which the masters pieced together the stern mosaics of San Marco. A noble seldom finds his way into the Ghetto. Only when the Jewish maidens gather at the well, one may sometimes notice a figure, black, in cloak and mask. Certain people know by experience that this figure carries a dagger hidden in those folds. Somebody is supposed to have seen the young man's face once in the moonlight, and since then they declare this dark slim visitor to be Marcantonio Priuli, son of the Proveditore Niccolò Priuli and the beautiful Caterina Minelli. It is known that he waits under the porch of Isaac Rosso's house; then, when people are gone, walks straight across the square and enters the house of old Melchizedek, the wealthy goldsmith, who has many sons and seven daughters and by his sons and daughters many grandchildren. Esther, the youngest granddaughter, awaits him, leaning against her aged grandsire's shoulder, in a low, dark chamber in which many objects glitter and glow, and silk and velvet hangs soft over the costly vessels, as though to quench their full, golden flames.

Here Marcantonio sits on a silver-embroidered cushion at the feet of the venerable Jew and tells of Venice, as he would tell a fairy-tale that never anywhere happened quite like that. He tells of the theater, of battles fought by the Venetian army, of foreign visitors, of pictures and statues, of the 'Sensa' on Ascension Day, of the Carnival, and of the beauty of his mother Caterina Minelli. All these have for him much the same meaning, being different expressions of power and love and life. To his two listeners it is all strange; for the Jews are strictly excluded from all society but their own, and even the wealthy old Melchizedek never sets foot within the domain of the Great Council, although as a goldsmith and because of the general respect in which he is held, he might have dared to do so. In the course of his long life, the old man had obtained from the Great Council many privileges for his co-religionists, who looked upon him as a father; but again and again he had had to endure the rebound. Every time a calamity befell the state, vengeance was taken on the Jews. The Venetians themselves were much too kin with them in spirit to use them, as other nations did, for commercial purposes; they plagued them with taxes, robbed them of their possessions, and restricted the boundary of the Ghetto more and more, so that the Jewish families, which in the midst of all their hardships increased fruitfully, were forced to build their houses up into the air, one upon the roof of the other. And their city, which did not lie by the sea, thus slowly grew up into the sky as into another sea, and around the square with the well the steep buildings rose on all sides like the walls of some giant tower.

The wealthy Melchizedek, in the eccentricity of old age, had made an odd proposal to his fellow-citizens, sons, and grandsons. He wished always to inhabit whichever was the highest of these tiny houses pushing upward, one above the other, in countless storeys. This strange desire was readily granted, for no one trusted the sustaining power of the lower walls anyway and such light bricks were set upon them that the wind did not seem to notice the walls at all. So the old man would move two or three times a year, and Esther, who refused to leave him, always with him. In the end they were so high that when they stepped from the confinement of their room out upon the flat roof, there began at the level of their eyes another country, of the customs of which the old man would speak in dark words, half psalmodizing. It was a long way up to them now; through the lives of many strangers, over steep and slippery steps, past scolding women and 'the onslaughts of hungry children that way led, and its many obstacles restricted all intercourse. Even Marcantonio no longer came to visit, and Esther hardly missed him. In the hours when she had been alone with him, she had looked at him so large-eyed and so long that it seemed to her he had plunged deep into her dark eyes and died, and that now there was beginning, in herself, his new, everlasting life, in which he as a Christian had of course believed. With this new feeling in her young body, she would stand all day on the roof, seeking the sea. But high though her house might be, there were only to be seen the gable of the Palazzo Foscari, some tower or other, the cupola of a church, a more distant cupola that seemed to shiver in the light, and then a lattice of masts, beams, poles against the rim of the humid, quivering sky.

Towards the end of that summer the old man, though the climbing was already hard for him despite all protest moved once more; for a new hut, high above all, had been built. As he crossed the square again after so long a time, leaning on Esther's arm, people gathered round him and bent low over his fumbling hands and begged for his advice in many matters; for he was to them like one dead who rises from his grave because a certain time is fulfilled. And so indeed it seemed. The men told him that there was revolt in Venice, the nobles were in danger, and soon the boundaries of the Ghetto would fall and all would enjoy the same freedom. The old man answered nothing, and only nodded as though all this had long been known to him and much more besides. He entered the house of Isaac Rosso, on the very top of which his new abode was perched, and spent half a day climbing the stairs.

Up there Esther bore a delicate, blond child. When she had recovered, she took it in her arms out upon the roof and for the first time let its open eyes be filled with the whole golden sky. It was an autumn morning of indescribable clearness. Things had a dusky look, almost without luster, only now and then flying lights would settle on them, as on large blossoms, rest a while and then soar away over the golden line of their contours into the sky. And there, where they disappeared, one caught sight from this highest spot of that which no one had ever seen from the Ghetto before —a still and silvery light: the sea. And only now, when Esther's eyes had grown accustomed to the glory, did she notice, at the roof's very edge, Melchizedek. He rose with outspread arms, forcing his dim eyes to gaze into the slowly unfolding day. His arms remained uplifted, a radiant thought upon his brow; it was as though he were offering a sacrifice. Then he leaned forward again and again and pressed his venerable head upon the rough, jagged stones. The people stood assembled on the square below, gazing up at him. Here and there words and gestures rose out of the crowd, but they did not reach to the old man praying in solitude. And the people saw their oldest and their youngest as in the clouds. The old man continued, rising proudly to his feet and then anew falling prostrate in humility; for a long time he continued. And the crowd below grew and did not let him out of their sight: Had he seen the sea or God, the eternal, in his glory?"

Herr Baum endeavored to say something quickly. But he did not at once succeed. "The sea probably," he then said dryly; "it really *is* impressive"—whereby he showed himself to be particularly enlightened and sensible.

I hastily bade him good-bye, but I could not refrain from calling after him: "Don't forget to tell your children this incident."

He thought a moment: "The children? But you know, that young nobleman, that Antonio or whatever his name is, he is not at all a nice character, and then the baby—that baby! That seems rather—for children—"

"Oh," I reassured him, "you have forgotten, my dear sir, that all babies come from God. Why should the children wonder that Esther had one, since she lived so near the sky!"

This story too the children have heard, and when you ask them what *they* think it may have been that the old Jew Melchizedek saw in his ecstasy, they say without stopping to think:

"Oh, the sea too."

Of One Who
Listened to the Stones

≫≪

I AM with my lame friend again. He smiles in his characteristic way:

"And about Italy you have never told me yet."

"Which means I am to make up for it as soon as I can?"

Ewald nods and has already closed his eyes to listen. So I begin:

"What we feel as spring, God sees as a fleeting little smile passing over the earth. Earth seems to be remembering something; in summer she tells every one about it, until she grows wiser in the great autumnal silence, through which she confides in those who are lonely. All the springs you and I have lived through, put together, still do not suffice to fill a single one of God's seconds. A spring, for God to notice it, may not remain in trees and on the meadows; it must somehow manifest its strength in man, for then it will proceed, as it were, not within time, but rather in eternity and in God's presence.

Once when this happened, God's glances must have been hovering in their dark wings over Italy. The country down there was bathed in light, the century itself shining like gold, but right across it, like a dark path, lay the shadow of a sturdy man, heavy and black, and far before it the shadow of his creating hands, restless, twitching, now over Pisa, now over Naples, now dissolving over the vague motion of the sea. God could not take his eyes from those hands, which at first seemed to him folded, like praying hands—but the prayer that welled forth from them forced them far apart.

A silence fell in the heavens. All the saints followed God's gaze and like him watched the shadow that hid half Italy, and the hymns of the angels froze upon their lips, and the stars trembled, for they feared to have done some wrong, and waited humbly for God's angry word. But nothing of the kind happened. The heavens had opened in their whole breadth over Italy, so that Raphael was on his knees in Rome while the blessed Fra Angelico of Fiesole stood on a cloud and rejoiced over him. Many prayers were at that hour on their way from the earth. But God recognized only one thing: the strength of Michelangelo rose up to him like fragrance of vineyards. And he suffered it to fill his thoughts. He bent lower, found the striving man, looked beyond his shoulder at the hands that hovered listening about the stone, and started: Did the very stones have souls? Why was this man listening to the stones? And now the hands awoke and tore at the stone as at a grave, in which a faint, dying voice is flickering. 'Michelangelo,' cried God in dread, 'who is in that stone?' Michelangelo listened; his hands were trembling. Then he answered in a muffled voice: 'Thou, my God, who else? But I cannot reach Thee.' And then God sensed that he was indeed *in the stone*, and he felt fearful and confined. The whole sky was but a stone, and he locked in its midst, hoping for the hands of Michelangelo to deliver him; and he heard them coming, though as yet afar.

But the master was at work again. He thought continually: 'Thou art but a little block, and some one else might scarcely find *one* figure in thee. But I feel a shoulder here: it is that of Joseph of Arimathaea; and here Mary bends down: I sense the trembling of her hands that support Jesus, Our Lord, who has just died on the cross. If in this little block of marble there is room for these three, why should I not sometime lift a whole sleeping race out of a rock?'

And with broad strokes he set free the three figures of the Pietà, but he did not lift the veils of stone entirely from their faces, as though he feared that their deep sorrow might lay a numbness on his hands. So he fled to another stone. But each time he lacked courage to give a brow its full serenity, a shoulder its perfect curve, nor when he made a woman did he lay the ultimate smile about her lips, lest her beauty might be all betrayed.

At this time he was designing the monument for Julius della Rovere. He thought to build a mountain over the Iron Pope, and a race of men therewith, to people the mountain. Filled with many dim plans, he went out to his marble quarries. The mountainside rose steep above a poor village. Surrounded by olive trees and weather-beaten rock, the newly-broken surfaces of stone appeared like a great pale face under ageing hair. Long Michelangelo stood before

77

that veiled brow. Suddenly he perceived below it two enormous eyes of stone, watching him. And Michelangelo felt his own stature grow under the influence of that look. Now he too towered over the land; it seemed to him that since the beginning of time he and this mountain had been brothers. The valley receded below him as under one climbing, the little huts crowded together like herds of cattle, and the great face of rock under its white stone veils appeared ever nearer and more kin. It had a waiting expression, motionless and yet on the verge of motion.

Michelangelo pondered: 'Thou canst not be hewn asunder, for thou indeed art but one.' And then he lifted up his voice: 'Thee will I complete, thou art my task.' And he turned back towards Florence. He saw a star and the tower of the Duomo. And about his feet was evening.

Of a sudden, at the Porta Romana, he hesitated. The two rows of houses reached out towards him like arms, and already they had taken hold of him and were drawing him into the town. And ever narrower and more dusky the streets became, and as he entered his house, he knew himself to be in mysterious hands, from which he could not escape. He fled into the hall and thence into the low chamber, scarcely two paces long, in which he was wont to write. Its walls leaned upon him, and it was as though they fought with his enormousness and forced him back into his old, restricted form. And he endured it. He fell upon his knees and let himself be shaped by them. He felt a never-known humility within him, and himself longed somehow to be small.

And there came a voice: 'Michelangelo, who is in

thee?' And the man in the narrow chamber laid his head heavily upon his hands and softly said: 'Thou, my God, who else?'

And all became wide around God, and he freely lifted up his face, that was over Italy, and looked about him: in mantles and miters the saints stood there, and the angels with their songs, as with vessels filled at radiant springs, went about among the thirsting stars, and to the heavens there was no end."

My lame friend looked up and suffered the evening clouds to draw his gaze with them along the sky.

"But is God t h e r e?" he asked.

I was silent. Then I bent towards him: "Ewald, are we really h e r e?"

And warmly we clasped hands.

How the Thimble
Came to Be God

≫≪

WHEN I stepped away from the window, the evening clouds were still there. They seemed to be waiting. Should I tell them a story too? I proposed it. But they didn't even hear me. To make myself understood and to diminish the distance between us, I called out: "I am an evening cloud too." They stopped still, evidently taking a good look at me. Then they stretched towards me their fine, transparent, rosy wings. That is how evening clouds greet each other. They had recognized me.

"We are lying over the earth," they explained, "more exactly, over Europe. And you?"

I hesitated. "There's a country here—"

"What does it look like?" They inquired.

"Well," I answered, "twilight, with things—"

"Europe's like that too," laughed a young girl-cloud.

"Possibly," I said, "but I have always heard that the things in Europe are dead."

"Yes, of course!" said another cloud scornfully. "What nonsense that would be—living things!"

"All the same," I insisted, "mine are alive. So that's the

difference. They can become various things, and one that comes into the world as a pencil or a stove, need not yet despair on that account of advancing in life. A pencil may someday turn into a staff, or, if all goes well, into a mast; and a stove at least into a city gate."

"You seem to me to be a very simpleminded evening cloud," said the youngster who had already expressed herself with so little reserve.

An old man-cloud feared she might have offended me. "There are all sorts of countries," he said kindly. "I once chanced to come over a small German principality, and I've never to this day believed that that belonged to Europe."

I thanked him and said: "I see it will not be easy for us to come to an understanding. Allow me, and I will simply tell you what I saw below me recently; that will probably be the best way."

"Please do," agreed the wise old man-cloud in the name of all the rest.

I began: "People are in a room. I am fairly high up, you must know, and so it is that to me they look like children; therefore I shall simply say: children. So then: Children are in a room. Two, five, six, seven children. It would take too long to ask them their names. Besides, they seem to be having an earnest discussion, so there's a good chance that a name or two will be given away in the course of it. They must have been at it for some time already, for the eldest (I observe that they call him Hans) is saying in a tone of finality:

'No it certainly cannot remain like this. I have heard that parents used always to tell their children stories in the

evening—or at least on evenings when they had been good
—till they went to sleep. Does anything like that happen
now?' A short pause, then Hans answered himself: 'It
doesn't happen, anywhere. I for my part—and also because
I'm fairly grown-up—would gladly let them off those few
wretched dragons that would bother them so, but still, they
should by rights tell us there are fairies, brownies, princes,
and monsters.'

'I have an aunt,' a little girl remarked, 'and she sometimes tells me . . .'

'Oh, go on,' Hans cut her off, 'aunts don't count, *they*
tell lies.' The whole assembly was much taken aback by this
bold, but uncontradicted assertion. Hans went on: 'Besides,
we are above all concerned with our parents, for it is their
duty, in a way, to instruct us in these matters; others do it
more out of kindness, we can't expect it of them. But just listen now: what do our parents do? They go around with
cross, annoyed faces, nothing suits them, they shout and
scold, and yet they are really so indifferent that if the world
came to an end they would hardly notice it. They have something which they call "Ideals." Perhaps those are some sort of
small children that may never be left alone and that make
a lot of trouble; but then they shouldn't have had *us!* Well,
I think it's like this, children: that our parents neglect us
is sad, certainly. But we would put up with that if it were
not a sign that grown-ups generally are growing stupider,
deteriorating, if one may say so. We cannot hinder their
decline; for all day long we cannot exert any influence on
them, and when we come home late from school, nobody
will expect us to sit down and try to get them interested in

something sensible. And it really does hurt when one has been sitting and sitting under the lamp and Mother cannot even understand the Pythagorean proposition. Well, that's how it is. So the grown-ups will be growing stupider and stupider . . . no matter: what can we lose by it? Culture? They take off their hats to each other, but if a bald spot comes to light, they laugh. Anyhow, they're always laughing. If we hadn't sense enough to cry now and then, even these matters would get entirely out of balance. And they're so arrogant: they even declare that the Emperor is a grown-up. I've read in the newspapers that the King of Spain is a child, and it's the same with all kings and emperors—don't let them talk you into anything! But apart from everything superfluous they've got, the grown-ups have something that most certainly cannot be indifferent to us—I mean, God. I've not seen him with any one of them yet—but that's just what looks suspicious. It has occurred to me that in their distraction and fuss and haste they may have lost him somewhere. But he is something absolutely necessary. All sorts of things can't happen without him: the sun can't rise, babies can't come, and even bread would stop; even if it does come out of the baker's, God sits and turns the big mills. It is easy to find lots of reasons why God is something we cannot do without. But this much is certain: the grown-ups aren't bothering about him, so we children must do it. Listen to a plan I've thought out. There are just seven of us children. Each of us must carry God about with him for one day, then he will be with us the whole week and we shall always know where he is at the moment.'

Here arose a great embarrassment. How was that to

be done? Could one take God into one's hand or put him in one's pocket? Then a little boy said:

'Once I was all alone in the room. A little lamp burned beside me and I sat up in bed and said my evening prayer —very loud. Something moved inside my folded hands. It was soft and warm and like a little bird. I couldn't open my hands, because the prayer wasn't over. But I wanted very badly to know and I prayed awfully fast. When I got to the Amen, I went like this' (the little boy stretched out his hands and spread out his fingers) 'but there was nothing there.'

This they could all picture to themselves. Even Hans had no suggestion. They were all looking at him. And then he suddenly said: 'How stupid! Any thing can be God. One has only to tell it.' He turned to the red-haired boy standing next him. 'An animal can't do that. It runs away. But a thing, you see, stays where it is; you come into the room, by day, by night: it is always there, it can very well be God.' Gradually the others became convinced of this. 'But we need a small object,' he continued, 'something one can carry with one everywhere, otherwise it's no good. Empty all your pockets.'

At that some very strange things appeared: scraps of paper, penknives, erasers, feathers, bits of string, pebbles, screws, whistles, chips of wood, and much else not to be distinguished from this distance or for which I lack a name. And all these things lay in the children's shallow hands, as though frightened at the sudden possibility of turning into God, while any of them that could shine a little, shone in order to please Hans. The choice hung in the balance a long time. At last there was found in little Resi's possession a thimble which she had taken from her mother one day. It was bright, as though made of silver, and for its beauty's sake it became God. Hans himself put into his pocket, for he had the first turn, and the other children followed him about all day long and were proud of him. Only it was hard to agree on who should have it next day, so Hans in his foresight then and there drew up the program for the whole week, so that no quarrel should break out.

This arrangement proved on the whole thoroughly expedient. One could see at first glance who had God. For that particular child walked rather more stiffly and solemnly and wore a Sunday face. For the first three days, the children spoke of nothing else. At every instant one of them was asking to see God, and though the thimble hadn't changed a whit under the influence of its great dignity, the thimblyness of it now seemed but a modest dress about its real form. Everything proceeded as arranged. On Wednesday Paul had it, on Thursday little Anna. Then came Saturday. The children were playing tag and romping in breathless confusion, when Hans suddenly called out: 'Who has God now?' They all stood still. Each looked at the other. Nobody remembered having seen him for the last two days. Hans counted off whose turn it was; the fact came out: it was little Marie's. And now they were asking little Marie without more ado to produce God. What was she to do? The little girl scratched around in her pockets. Then only did she remember that he had been given to her in the morning; and now he was gone—she had probably lost him here while playing.

And when all the other children went home, little Marie stayed behind on the green, searching. The grass was fairly high. Twice people passed and asked whether she had lost anything. Each time the child answered: 'A thimble' —and went on looking. The people helped her for a time, but soon tired of stooping, and one man advised as he left: 'You had better go home now, you can always buy a new one.'

But still little Marie went on searching. The meadow grew more and more mysterious in the dusk, and the grass began to get wet. Then another man came along. He bent over the child: 'What are you looking for?' This time little Marie, not far from tears but brave and defiant, replied: 'I am looking for God.' The stranger smiled and took her simply by the hand, and she let herself be led as though all were well now. On the way the stranger said: 'And just look, what a beautiful thimble I found today!'—"

The evening clouds had long been impatient. Then the wise old man-cloud, who had grown fat in the meantime, turned to me:

"Pardon me, but may I ask what the country is called —over which you . . . ?"

But the other clouds ran laughing into the sky and dragged the old fellow along with them.

A Tale of Death
and a Strange Postscript Thereto

𝕾𝕶

I WAS still gazing up into the slowly fading evening sky, when some one said: "You seem to be very much interested in that country up there?"

My glance fell quickly, as if shot down, and I realized: I had come to the low wall of our little churchyard, and before me, on the other side of it, stood the man with the spade, sagely smiling.

"*I'm* interested in *this* country here," he went on, pointing to the black, damp earth appearing here and there between the many dead leaves that rustled as they stirred, while I did not know a wind had sprung up. Suddenly I exclaimed, seized with a violent aversion: "Why do you do that?"

The gravedigger still smiled. "It is a way of earning one's bread—and besides, I ask you, aren't most people doing the same? They bury God *up there* as I bury men here." He pointed to the sky and explained to me: "Yes, that too is a great grave, in summer it is covered with wild forget-me-nots—"

I interrupted him: "There was a time when men buried

God in the sky, that is true—"

"And is it any different now?" he asked, curiously sad.

I went on: "It used to be customary for every one to throw a handful of sky over him, I know. But even then he really wasn't there any more, or at least—" I hesitated.

"You know," I began again, "in olden times people prayed like this—" and I spread my arms out wide, involuntarily feeling my breast expand at the gesture. "In those days God would cast himself into all these human abysses, full of despair and darkness, and only reluctantly did he return into his heavens, which, unnoticed, he drew down ever closer over the earth. But a new faith began. As it could not make men understand wherein its new God differed from their old one (for as soon as they began to praise him, men promptly recognized the one old God here too), the promulgator of the new commandment changed the manner of praying. He taught the folding of hands and declared: "See, *thus* does our God wish to be implored, so he must be another God from the one whom heretofore you have thought to receive into your arms.' The people saw this, and the gesture of open arms became a despicable and dreadful one, and later it was fastened to the cross that all might see in it a symbol of agony and death.

Now when God next looked down upon the earth, he was frightened. Besides the many folded hands, many Gothic cathedrals had been built, and so the hands and the roofs, alike steep and sharp, stretched pointing towards him like the weapons of an enemy. With God there is a different bravery. He turned back into his heavens, and when he saw that the steeples and the new prayers were growing in pur-

suit of him, he departed out of his domain at the other side
and thus eluded the chase. He was himself astonished to
find, out beyond his radiant home, a beginning darkness
that received him silently, and with a curious feeling he
went on and on in this dusk that reminded him of the hearts
of men. Then for the first time it occurred to him that the
heads of men are lucid, but their hearts full of a similar darkness; and a longing came over him to dwell in the hearts of
men and no longer to move through the clear, cold wakeful-
ness of their thinking. Well, God has continued on his way.
Ever denser grows the darkness around him, and the night
through which he presses on has something of the fragrant
warmth of fecund clods of earth. And in a little while the
roots will reach out towards him with the old beautiful
gesture of wide prayer. There is nothing wiser than the
circle. The God who has fled from us out of the heavens,
out of the earth will he come to us again. And, who knows,
perhaps you yourself will some day dig free the door . . ."

The man with the spade said: "But that is a fairy-tale."

"In the words with which we speak," I answered
gently, "everything becomes a fairy-tale, for in them it can
never have happened."

The man stared for a while, reflecting. Then with im-
petuous gestures he pulled on his coat, asking: "We can go
together, can't we?"

I nodded: "I'm going home. I daresay we go the same
way. But don't you live here?"

He stepped through the little latticed gate, swung it
gently to on its plaintive hinges, and answered, "No."

After a few steps, he grew more confidential: "You

were quite right just now," he said. "It is strange that any-one can be found who wants to do that job back there. I never used to think about it. But now, since I'm growing older, thoughts come to me sometimes, singular thoughts, like that about the sky, and others too. Death. What do we know of it? Apparently everything and perhaps nothing. Often children (I don't know whom they belong to) stand round me as I work. And then I get one of those ideas. I dig like a wild beast, so as to draw all my strength away from my brain and use it up in my arms. The grave gets much deeper than the regulations call for, and a mountain of earth rises beside it. But the children run away when they see my wild movements. They think I am angry for some reason." He pondered. "And it is a kind of anger. You grow callous, you think you've got the better of it, and then sud-denly. . . . It's no good; death is something incomprehensi-ble, terrible."

We were following a long road under fruit trees al-ready quite leafless, and on our left the forest began, like a night that might at any moment engulf us.

"I would like to relate to you a little story," I said tentatively; "it's just long enough to last us till we get there."

The man nodded and lighted his old stub of a pipe. I began:

"There were two people, a man and a woman, and they loved each other. To love is to accept nothing, from anywhere, to forget everything and to want to receive everything from one person, both that which one already had and all else. That was the mutual wish of these two. But in the realm of time, by day, among the many, where so much comes and goes, often before one has got into real touch with it, it is not at all possible to carry through such loving; events rush in from all sides, and chance opens every door to them.

For this reason the two decided to leave the daily world and go into solitude, far away from the striking of clocks and the noises of the city. And there, in a garden, they built themselves a house. And the house had two doors, one on its right side and one on its left. And the right-hand door was the man's door, and everything that was his was to pass through it into the house. The door on the left was the woman's door, and all that she cared about was to enter that way. And so it was. The one who woke first in the morning, went down and opened his door. And so until late at night a very great deal indeed came in, even though the house was not on the edge of the road. To those who know how to receive, the landscape comes into a house and the light and a breeze with a fragrance about its shoulders, and much more besides. But past things also, figures, destinies, came in by both these doors, and all were welcomed with the like simple hospitality, so that they felt as though they had always been at home in the house on the heath. This went on for a long time and the two were very happy because of it. The door at the left was opened rather more often, but by the right-hand door entered more motley guests. And before the first door one morning waited —Death. The man slammed his door quickly shut when he noticed him, and kept it tightly bolted all day long. After some time, Death appeared at the door on the left. Trembling, the woman flung it to and shot the broad bolt home.

They did not speak to each other of this occurrence, but they opened both doors less often and tried to get along with what they had in the house. Of course they had to live much more meagerly than before. Their provisions grew scarce, and cares set in. They both began to sleep badly; and in one of those long, wakeful nights, they both at once suddenly heard a strange shuffling and knocking noise. It came from outside the house wall, equally far from the two doors, and sounded as though some one were beginning to break out the stones in order to make a new door midway in the wall. Even in their terror the two pretended they did not notice anything unusual. They began to talk, to laugh unnaturally loud, and when they were tired out, the rummaging in the wall had stopped. Since then both the doors have remained closed. The two live like prisoners. Their health is failing and they have strange fancies. The noise is repeated from time to time. Then they laugh with their lips, while their hearts almost die of fear. And they both know that the burrowing is getting always louder and clearer, and they must talk and laugh louder and louder with their always wearier voices."

I ceased.

"Yes, yes—" said my companion, "so it is; that is a true story."

"I read this one in an old book," I went on to add, "and a very curious thing happened when I was doing so. At the end of the line which tells how Death came also to the woman's door, there had been drawn in old and faded ink a little star. It peeped out from between the words as between clouds, and for a moment I fancied that, were the lines to draw apart, they might reveal a lot of stars standing there behind them, as does sometimes happen when the spring sky clears late of an evening. Then I forgot all about the insignificant circumstance, until one day, on the smooth, glossy paper inside the back cover of the book, I found, as though mirrored in a lake, the same little star, and close beneath it delicate lines began which flowed away like waves over the pale, reflecting surface. The writing had become blurred in many places, but still I was able to decipher nearly all of it. It said something of this sort:

'I have read this story so often, on all possible kinds of days, that I sometimes believe I have written it down myself, out of my own memory. But for me it goes on as I set it down here:

'The woman had never seen Death; in all innocence she let him enter. But Death said, rather hurriedly and as one whose conscience is not clear: "Give this to your husband." And he added quickly, as she looked inquiringly at him: "It is seed, very good seed." Then he went away without looking back. The woman opened the little sack he had pressed into her hand; there really were seeds of some kind in it, hard, ugly grains. And the woman thought: "A seed is something incomplete, belonging to the future. One cannot tell what will come of it. I won't give my husband these unsightly grains; they don't look in the least like a gift. Rather will I tuck them in the flowerbed in our garden and wait to see what grows out of them. Then I will lead him to the plant and tell him how I came by it." And so the woman did. And they continued to live as before. The man, who could not forget that Death had stood before his portal, was at first somewhat uneasy, but when he saw the woman as hospitable and care-free as ever, he too soon opened the wide wings of his door again, so that much life and light came into the house.

'The following spring there stood in the middle of the bed among the slender tiger-lilies, a small shrub. It had narrow, blackish leaves, rather pointed, like those of the laurel, and a peculiar gleam lay on their dark surface. Every day the man intended to ask whence the plant had sprung. But every day he failed to do so. In a similar reticence the woman from day to day withheld her explanation. But the suppressed question on the one side and the never-ventured answer on the other, drew the two together often before the little shrub, the green darkness of which contrasted so strangely with the garden. When the next spring came, they busied themselves with the shrub as much as with the other plants, and they were saddened when, surrounded by so much growing bloom, it came up unchanged and mute as in the first year, insensible to all sun. Then it was that they determined, without telling each other, to devote all their energy in the third spring to this plant, and as that spring appeared, they tenderly fulfilled, and hand in hand, what each had promised to himself. The garden all around grew wild, and the tiger-lilies seemed paler than usual. But once, as after a night heavy and overcast, they stepped out into the garden, the quiet, shimmering morning garden, they saw that from the sharp black leaves of the strange shrub, a pale blue flower had sprung unscathed, bursting now the too-close sheath about its bud. And they stood before it united and silent, and now they knew less than ever what to say. For they were thinking: "Now is Death flowering," and together they bent down to savor the fragrance of the young bloom.—And since that morning everything has been different in the world.' This is what it said," I concluded, "inside the cover of the old book."

"And who would have written it?" urged the grave-digger.

"A woman, by the handwriting," I replied. "But what good would it have done to find out? The characters were very faded and rather old-fashioned. Probably she had long been dead."

My companion was lost in thought. "Only a story," he admitted at last, "and yet it touches one so."

"Ah, that is if one doesn't hear stories often," I said soothingly.

"You think so?" He gave me his hand and I held it fast. "But I would like so much to repeat it. May I?"

I nodded. Then he suddenly remembered:

"But I have no one. Whom should I tell it to?"

"Oh, that's easy. "Tell it to the children who sometimes come to watch you. Whom else?"

And the children have really heard the last three stories. That is, the one repeated by the evening clouds only in part, if I am correctly informed. The children are small, of course, and so they are much further from the evening clouds than we. But in the case of *that* story this is just as well. For in spite of Hans's long, well-worded speech, they would realize that the affair took place among children, and as experts would look upon my telling of it critically. But it is better that they should not learn with what effort and how awkwardly we experience the things that happen quite simply and so naturally to them.

A Society Sprung
of an Urgent Need

⚜

I HAVE just learned that our town also possesses a kind of artists' club. It recently came into being to meet a need that was, as one may easily imagine, very urgent, and rumor goes that it "flourishes." When societies are at a loss what to do with themselves, they flourish; they have heard that one must do this in order to be a proper society.

Needless to say, Herr Baum is Honorary Member, Founder, Flagfather and everything else in one and the same person, and has some difficulty in keeping these various dignities apart. He sent me a young man with an invitation to attend the club's "Evenings." I thanked him most politely, as goes without saying, but added that my entire activity during some five years past had consisted in doing the very opposite.

"Picture to yourself," I explained with appropriate seriousness, "since that time hardly a moment has passed during which I have not been resigning, stepping out of some association or other, and yet there are still societies which, so to speak, contain me."

The young man looked startled at first, and then, with

an expression of respectful pity at my feet. He must have seen in them confirmation of my "steppings out," for he nodded his head understandingly. That pleased me well, and as I had to leave at that moment, I suggested that he accompany me a little way. So we walked through the town and on beyond, towards the station, for I had business in the neighborhood. We talked about a variety of things; I learned that the young man was a musician. He told me so, modestly; one would never have guessed it. Aside from the profusion of his hair, he was marked by a great, an almost bounding readiness to help. During our not particularly long walk, he twice picked up one of my gloves, held my umbrella for me while I looked for something in my pockets, blushingly drew my attention to the fact that there was something sticking to my beard and a smut on my nose; and his thin fingers lengthened the while, as though they longed to approach my face helpfully in this way. In his zeal the young man even dropped back from time to time and removed from the bushes, with evident enjoyment, dead leaves that in fluttering down had caught among the twigs. I foresaw that through these repeated delays I should miss my train (we were still some way from the station), and I decided to tell my companion a story to hold him awhile at my side. I began without further preliminaries:

"I know how things went with one of those societies, one for which there was a real necessity. You shall see. Not so very long ago, three artists met by chance in an old town. The three artists naturally did *not* talk about art. At least, so it appeared. They spent the evening in the back room of an ancient inn, exchanging tales of their travel adventures and experiences of all sorts. Their stories became shorter and shorter and more and more literal as time went on, and finally they had got down to a couple of jokes which they kept on bandying back and forth. To forestall any misunderstanding, I must also say at once that they were real artists, intended to be so by Nature, as it were, not by chance. This evening squandered in the back room of an inn cannot alter the fact; and we shall presently see what came of it. Other people, philistines, came to this inn; the artists were discomfited and left. The moment they passed out of the door they were changed men. They walked in the middle of the street, a little separated from each other. Their countenances still showed traces of their recent laughter, that strange disorder of the features, but the eyes of all three were already serious and observant. Suddenly the one in the middle nudged the one on the right, who understood at once.

Before them lay an alley, narrow, full of tenuous, warm twilight. It mounted slightly, which gave a very telling perspective, and there was something uncommonly secretive about it and yet again intimate. The three artists gave themselves up to the impression for a moment. They did not speak, for they knew one cannot *say* that sort of thing. They had, after all, become artists because there is much one cannot say. Suddenly the moon rose somewhere, picking out a single gable in silver, and a song floated up from a courtyard. 'Striving for effect—!' growled the artist in the middle, and they went on.

They were walking a little closer together now, though they still took up the whole width of the street. So they came unexpectedly upon a square. This time it was the artist on the right who drew the attention of the others. In this broader, more open scene, there was nothing disturbing about the moonlight; on the contrary, it was a downright necessity that it should be there. It made the square look larger, gave the houses a surprising, expectantly listening life; and the flat illuminated expanse of the pavement was audaciously broken in the middle by a fountain and its heavy cast shadow, a boldness which exceptionally impressed the artists. They stood close together, sucking, as it were, at the breasts of this mood. But they were unpleasantly interrupted. Light, hastening footsteps drew near; out of the darkness of the fountain a man's form materialized, welcomed the footsteps and what else belonged to them, with the customary tenderness—and the beautiful square had suddenly become a wretched magazine illustration from which the three painters turned as *one* painter. 'There's that damned novelistic element again!' shouted the one on the right, denoting by this correctly technical term the lovers at the fountain.

United in their resentment, the three wandered aimlessly round the town for a long time, continually discovering subjects, but each time enraged afresh by the way in which some banal incident or other ruined the quiet and simplicity of every picture. About midnight, they were sitting together at the inn, in the bedroom of the leftermost, the youngeest, and had no thought of going to bed. Their nocturnal stroll had roused many plans and projects in their minds, and having shown them at the same time that they were at bottom *one* in spirit, they were now, intensely interested, exchanging points of view. They cannot be said to have expressed themselves in faultless sentences; they cast about them with a few words no uninitiated person would have grasped, but they understood each other so well by this means that nobody in the adjoining rooms could get to sleep until towards four o'clock in the morning.

Now this long confabulation had a real, a visible result. Something in the nature of a society was founded; that is, it really had already existed the moment the aims and intentions of the three artists had proved so similar that one could only with difficulty separate them from each other. The first resolution of the 'Society' was promptly carried out. They traveled for three hours into the country and together rented a farm. Staying in town would have had no point at this juncture. Out there they intended first to acquire their 'style,' that particular personal certainty, the eye, the hand and whatever one calls all the things without which a painter may indeed live, but cannot paint. In the acquisition of all these virtues, coöperation—the 'Society' itself—was to help, and particularly the honorary member of this society: Nature. By "Nature", artists understand everything that God has made himself or might, under certain circumstances, have made. A fence, a house, a fountain —all these things are usually of human origin. But when they have been standing in the landscape for a time, so that they have taken on certain qualities from the trees and bushes and the rest of their surroundings, then they pass over, as it were, into God's possession and with that also into the domain of the painter. For God and the artist have the same riches and the same poverty, accordingly.

Now in the nature that lay stretched about this communal farmyard God surely did not think to possess any particular treasure. It did not take long, however, for the artists to teach him better. The country round was flat; that there was no denying. But through the depth of its shadows and the brilliance of its lights valleys and peaks were created, between which a countless number of intermediate tones corresponded to those areas of wide meadows and fertile fields that constitute the material wealth of a mountainous region. There were but few trees and almost all of the same species, botanically speaking. Through the emotions they expressed, however, through the longing of some spreading branch or the gentle reverence of some trunk, they seemed like a great number of individual beings and many a willow proved to be a personality which through the complexity and depth of its character provided the artists with one surprise after another. So great was their enthusiasm they felt so much at one in this work of theirs, it was of no moment that after six months each of the three had moved into a house of his own; that was surely just for reasons of space. But there is something else that must be mentioned here. The painters wanted to celebrate in some way the first anniversary of their society, out of which so much good had come in so short a time, and to this end each determined secretly to paint pictures of the houses of the other two.

On the appointed day they came together, each with his pictures. It so happened that they began to talk about their houses, how they were situated, how conveniently built, and the like. They became quite excited, and it turned out that in the course of the discussion each of them forgot the oil sketches he had brought along, so that each arrived home late at night with his unopened parcel. How this could have happened is hard to understand. Nor did they, during the next few weeks, show each other their pictures, and when one went to visit another (which as a consequence of much work happened more and more seldom) he found on his friend's easel sketches from that first period when they were still living together at the same farm.

One day, however, the one on the right (he was *living* on the right too now, so I shall continue to call him thus) came, in the studio of the one I have called the youngest, upon one of these unconfessed anniversary pictures aforementioned. He observed it thoughtfully for a time, then took it to the light and suddenly burst out laughing: 'Fancy, I never knew, and it's not a bad conception of my house you've given here. A truly clever caricature! With these exaggerations in form and color, with that bold interpretation of my gable—which certainly is rather emphasized—really, there's something in it!' The expression the face of the youngest took on was not one of his most becoming; on the contrary. In his consternation he went to see the middle one, the most sensible of the three, hoping to be reassured by him; for when this sort of thing happened to him he at once became despondent and inclined to doubt his own ability. His friend not being in when he arrived, he began poking around a little in the studio, when his eyes promptly fell upon a picture that peculiarly repelled him. It was a house, but a perfect fool must have lived in it. What a façade! It could only have been built by someone who had no idea of architecture and had applied his miserable painter's notions to a building. Suddenly the youngest shoved the picture away as though it had burnt his fingers. In its left-hand corner he had seen the date of that first anniversary and next it: 'The House of our Youngest.' Naturally he did not wait for his host's return, but went home somewhat out of humor.

After this he and his fellow on the right had become careful. They sought subjects far afield and of course did not dream of preparing anything against the second anniversary of their so promotive society. Their unsuspecting comrade in the middle worked all the more zealously at a subject that lay close to the house of the one on the right. Some vague sense kept him from choosing the house itself as the excuse for his picture.—When he brought him the finished product, his friend on the right seemed remarkably reticent, just glanced at it fleetingly and made some casual comment. Then, after a while, he said:

'I did not know you had been so far away lately.'

'How so, been away? Far?' The middle one didn't understand in the least.

'Well, that good bit of work there,' replied the other, 'evidently some Dutch motive or other—'

His sensible comrade of the middle laughed heartily. 'Excellent!' he exclaimed. 'That Dutch motive lies before your very door!' And he was not to be silenced.

But his brother-member did not laugh, not at all. He managed a wry smile and said: 'A good joke.'

'But not at all,' said the other. 'Just open the door and I'll show you—' and he started in that direction himself.

'Stop,' ordered the master of the house. 'I hereby declare to you that I have never seen that landscape and *never shall see it*, because to my eyes it is incapable of existing at all.'

'But—' the other expostulated, surprised.

'You insist?' shouted the painter of the right in his irritation. 'Well, then, I leave—and to-day. You force me to go, for I do not wish to live in such surroundings. Understand?'

That was the end of their friendship, but not of the society; for to this day it has not been statutorily dissolved. Nobody has thought of doing that, and it may with good reason be said of this society that it has spread over the whole world."

"It shows once more," interrupted the obliging young man, who had been thoughtfully screwing up his lips, "one of those marvelous results of coöperation; surely many an outstanding master has been produced by this intimate association—"

"Allow me," I begged, as without warning he dusted off my sleeve, "this was really but the introduction to my story, though it is more involved than the story itself. Well—I said the society has spread all over the world, and that is a fact. Its three members fled from each other in true horror. Nowhere could they find peace. Each lived in constant fear that one of the others might notice a piece of his country and profane it by his malicious presentation, and when they had arrived at three opposite points on the earth's periphery, the discomforting idea dawned upon each of them that his sky, the sky he had laboriously made his own through his growing originality, was still within reach of the others. In this shattering moment they began, all three at once, to go backwards with their easels, and five steps more and they would have fallen off the edge of the earth into infinity and would now be performing with frenzied speed the double revolution round the earth and round the sun. But God's sympathy and attentiveness averted this inhuman fate. God saw their danger, and at that last moment (what else should he have done?) he stepped out into the middle of the sky. The three painters started in astonishment. They fixed their easels and set up their palettes. They could not let this opportunity slip. God does not appear every day, nor yet to everybody. And of course each of the three thought God was standing to *him alone*. For the rest, they grew more and more engrossed in their interesting work. And every time God wants to go back into the sky again, Saint Luke begs him to stay out a while longer, until the three painters have finished their pictures."

"And doubtless the three gentlemen have already exhibited those pictures, perhaps even sold them?" asked the musician in the gentlest of tones.

"What are you thinking of?" I parried. "They are still painting away at God and they will probably go on painting him till they die themselves. And should they meet again in life (which I consider out of the question) and show each other the pictures they have meanwhile painted of God—who knows, perhaps those pictures would be scarcely distinguishable one from the other."

And now we had reached the station. I still had five minutes. I thanked the young man for accompanying me and wished him the best of success for the young society which he so well represented. With his right forefinger he flicked away the dust that seemed to weigh upon the windowsills in the little waiting-room, and he was rapt in thought. I must confess I was already flattering myself that my little story had put him into this reflective mood. When as a parting gesture he drew a red thread out of my glove, I counseled him in gratitude:

"You know, you can go back across the fields; it's considerably shorter that way than by the road."

"Pardon me," the obliging young man bowed, "I think I shall take the road again. I am trying to remember where it was: while you were being so good as to tell me some really important things, I thought I noticed a scarecrow in a field wearing an old coat, and one of the sleeves—seems to me it was the left—had caught on a stake so that it couldn't flap at all. Now I feel a certain duty to render my little tribute to the common interests of humanity—which I look upon as a kind of society too, in which everyone has something he should do—by restoring to that left sleeve its proper purpose, namely, to flap in the wind. . . ." The young man walked away with the most engaging smile. And I nearly missed my train.

Fragments of this story were sung by the young man at one of the club's "Evenings." God knows who contrived to set them to music for him. Herr Baum, the Flagfather, brought them home to the children, and the children have remembered some of the tunes.

The Beggar
and the Proud Young Lady

❧❧

IT HAPPENED that we—the schoolmaster and I—were witnesses to the following little incident. We have an old beggar who sometimes stands at the edge of the wood. Today too he was there again, poorer, more miserable than ever, almost indistinguishable, through a sort of sympathetic mimicry, from the boards of the rotted wooden fence against which he leaned. But then it happened that a very little girl came running up to give him a small coin. That in itself was not extraordinary; only the way she did it was surprising. She made her very best curtsy, tendered her little gift to the old man hurriedly, as though no one should see, curtsied again and was gone. But those two curtsies were worthy of at least an emperor. This annoyed our schoolmaster quite particularly. He started towards the beggar, probably to drive him from his fence-post; for, as we know, he was a director of the local charities and committed to the prevention of street-begging. I held him back.

"But," he protested, "we are helping these people, I may even go so far as to say we support them. And now if they beg on the streets, too, it's sheer—impertinence!"

"Dear Mister Schoolmaster—" I attempted to calm him, but he continued to drag me along towards the wood. "Dear Mister Schoolmaster," I besought him, "I must tell you a story."

"So urgently?" he asked venomously.

I took him up in all seriousness. "Yes, right away. Before you forget what we chanced to observe just now."

The schoolmaster mistrusted me after my last story. I read that in his face, and added in a conciliatory tone:

"Not about God, really not. God is not even mentioned in this story. It is something historical."

With that I had won. Just say the word "history," and every schoolmaster will prick up his ears; for history is something thoroughly respectable, has nothing captious about it and is often pedagogically useful. I noticed that the schoolmaster was polishing his glasses again, a sign that his powers of vision had shifted to his ears, and I made adroit use of this propitious moment. I began:

"It was in Florence. Lorenzo de' Medici, young, and not yet in power, had just composed his poem, 'Trionfo di Baccho ed Arianna,' and already it was echoing through all the gardens. Those were the days of living songs. Out of the darkness of the poet's soul they arose in men's voices and were wafted upon them, as on silver skiffs, fearless, into the unknown. The poet began a song, and all who sang it brought it to completion. In the 'Trionfo,' as in most songs of that time, life is celebrated—that violin with serene, singing strings and the dark background which is the stirring of our blood. Stanzas of uneven length mount upwards in a tumbling gaiety but each time, just at the point of breathlessness, a short simple refrain sets in, that bends down from the dizzy height and, fearing the abyss, seems to close its eyes. It runs:

> 'How lovely is youth, that delights us,
> Yet who would hold it? Youth flees and regrets,
> And if one would be merry, let him be so to-day,
> Of to-morrow there is no certainty.'

Is it to be wondered at that the men who sang such lines were overtaken by a haste, a striving to pile up all festivity tower-like on this to-day, upon the only rock on which it is worth while to build? Thus too can one explain the press of figures in the pictures of the Florentine painters, who sought to unite all their princes and their ladies and their friends in a *single* canvas; for painting was slow work, and who could know whether, when it came time for the next picture, all these people would still be so young and gay and friendly?

This spirit of impatience naturally found its clearest expression in the young men. The most brilliant of these were sitting together after a banquet on the terrace of the Palazzo Strozzi, discussing the performances shortly to take place before the church of Santa Croce. In a loggia a little apart from the rest stood Palla degli Albizzi with his friend Tomaso, the painter. They seemed to be arguing with increasing excitement, till Tomaso cried:

'That you never will do, I wager you never will!'

The others now took notice.

'What's the matter?' inquired Gaetano Strozzi, strolling up with some of his friends.

Tomaso explained: 'Palla says that at the festival he is going to kneel down before Beatrice Altichieri, that proud girl, and beg her to permit him to kiss the dusty hem of her robe.'

They all laughed, and Lionardo, of the house of Ricardi, said: 'Palla will think twice about that. He well knows that the fairest women have a smile for him which at other times one never sees upon their faces.'

Another added: 'And Beatrice is still so young. Her lips are still too childishly firm to smile. That is why she seems so proud.'

'No!' retorted Palla degli Albizzi with excessive vehemence. 'She *is* proud, but that is not the fault of her youth. She is proud as marble is in the hands of Michelangelo, proud as a flower in a picture of the Madonna, proud as a ray of sunlight passing over diamonds—'

Gaetano Strozzi interrupted him with some severity: 'And you, Palla, are not you proud also? To hear you, one would think you wanted to take your place among the beggars who wait about the hour of vespers in the court-yard of Santissima Annunziata, till Beatrice Altichieri passes and, with averted face, gives each of them a soldo."

'I will do even *that!*' cried Palla with blazing eyes, and pushing his friends aside, he sprang down the staircase and disappeared.

Tomaso was about to follow, but Strozzi held him back. 'Let be. He must be left to himself now; then he will come to his senses sooner.' And the young men dispersed into the gardens.

In the forecourt of Santissima Annunziata, that evening too, some twenty beggars, men and women, waited for vespers. Beatrice, who knew them all by name and would sometimes visit the children and the sick in their wretched homes at the Porta San Niccolò, used to present each one of them, in passing, with a small silver piece. To-day she seemed to be a little late; the bells had already rung their call, and only threads of their sound still hung about the towers above the darkening air. An uneasiness spread among the mendicants, also because a new beggar, a stranger, had slunk into the shadow of the porch, and they were about to drive him off in their jealousy, when a young girl in a black, almost nunnish dress, appeared in the fore-court and, hampered in her progress by her pitying kindness, went from one to the other, while one of her waiting-women held open the purse from which she took her little gifts. The beggars fell on their knees, sobbed, and sought to lay their shriveled fingers for one second on the train of their benefactress's simple gown, or kissed its bottom hem with their wet, stammering lips. She had passed them all, and not one of the figures so well known to her was missing. But suddenly she became aware under the shadow of the porch, of another figure in rags, a stranger. She was startled. She became confused. She had known all her poor friends as a child, and to help them had become as natural to her, as, say, the dipping of one's fingers in the marble font of holy water that stands at the entrance of every church. It had never occurred to her that there might be beggars one did not know. How should one have the right to give these something too, since one had not earned the confidence of their poverty by somehow knowing of it? Would it not

have been an unheard-of presumption to offer a stranger
alms? And filled with the conflict of these dark emotions,
the girl passed the new beggar by as though she had not
noticed him and stepped quickly into the cool, high church.
But inside, as the service began, she could not remember a
single prayer. A fear seized her that after vespers she might
no longer find the poor man in the porch, and she had done
nothing to alleviate his need, while the night was so near,
in which all poverty is sadder and more helpless than by
day. Signing to the one among her waiting-women who
carried her purse, she slipped out with her into the porch.
It had meantime been deserted; but the stranger still stood
there, leaning against a pillar, and seemed to listen to the
singing that came from the church, strangely remote, as if
from heavens. His face was almost entirely hidden, as is
sometimes the case with those lepers who do not uncover
their hideous sores until one stands close before them and
they are sure that pity and loathing will speak equally in
their favor. Beatrice hesitated. She was carrying the little
purse herself and felt that it contained only a few small
coins. But with a sudden resolve she went up to the beggar
and said, in an uncertain, slightly singsong voice, and without lifting her fugitive gaze from her own hands:

'I would not offend you, sir . . . I think, if I recognize you aright, I am in your debt. Your father, I believe,
made the fine balustrade in our house, of wrought-iron, you
know, that adorns the staircase. Later—they found—in the
room where he sometimes used to work—a purse—I think
he must have lost it—surely—'

But the helpless lie upon her lips forced the girl to her

knees before the stranger. She pressed the brocade purse into his hands, hidden in his cloak, and stammered: 'Forgive me—'

For an instant Beatrice felt the beggar tremble. Then she fled back into the church with her frightened waiting-woman. Through the briefly opened door there burst a short jubilant peal of voices.

That is the end of the story. Messer Palla degli Albizzi remained in his rags. He gave away all he had and went forth barefoot and destitute into the land. Later he is said to have lived near Subiaco."

"Oh, those times, those times!" said the schoolmaster. "What's the good of it all? He was on the way to becoming a profligate and through this incident he turned into a vagabond, an eccentric. I am sure nobody remembers him today."

"Oh, but they do," I ventured to contradict. "His name is mentioned now and then in the great litanies of the Catholic Church, among those intercessors to whom they pray, for he became a saint."

The children have heard this story too, and they declare, to the annoyance of the schoolmaster, that God does come into it. I am rather surprised at that myself, for I *had* promised the good schoolmaster to tell him a story without God in it. But, of course, the children must know!

A Story
Told to the Dark

≈≈

I WANTED to put on my coat and go to my friend
Ewald. But I had lingered over a book, an *old* book at that,
and evening had come, as in Russia spring comes. A moment
ago the room had been distinct, even to its remotest corners,
and now all the things in it acted as though they had never
known anything but twilight; everywhere large dark blossoms opened, and as on dragonfly wings a luminous gleam-
ing slipped about their velvet calyxes.

The lame man would surely no longer be at his window. So I stayed at home. What was it I had wanted to tell
him? I no longer knew. But after a while I felt that someone was entreating me for this lost story—some lonely soul,
perhaps, standing far away at the window of his dusky
room, or perhaps this very darkness itself that surrounded
me and him and all things. So it happened that I told my
story to the dark. And it leaned ever closer to me so that I
could speak more and more softly, quite as befits my story.
It takes place in the present, by the way, and begins:

"After a long absence Doctor Georg Lassmann was
returning to the simple home of his birth. He had never

possessed much there, and now he had only two sisters still living in his native city, both married, apparently well married; to see them again after twelve years was the purpose of his visit. So he himself believed. But in the night, unable to sleep in the overcrowded train, it became clear to him that he was really going for the sake of his childhood, hoping to rediscover something in those old streets: a doorway, a tower, a fountain, anything to induce some joy or some sorrow by which he might recognize himself again. One loses oneself so in life. And then he remembered many things: the little apartment in the Heinrichsgasse with the shiny doorknobs and the dark-coated tiles, the well-cared-for furniture and his parents, those two threadbare beings, standing almost reverently beside it; the hurrying and harassed week-days and the Sundays that were like cleared-out rooms, the rare visitors whom one received laughing and embarrassed, the out-of-tune piano, the old canary, the heirloom armchair in which one might not sit, a name-day, an uncle who came from Hamburg, a puppet-show, a barrel-organ, a children's party and someone calling: 'Klara.'

The doctor has almost dropped off. They are in a station, lights run by and the listening hammer goes ringing along the wheels. And that is like Klara, Klara. Klara, the doctor muses, now wide awake, who was Klara anyway? And next instant he becomes aware of a face, a child's face with blond, straight hair. Not that he could describe it, but he has a sense of something quiet, helpless, resigned, of a pair of narrow childish shoulders squeezed still more together by a washed-out little dress, and he begins to imagine a face to go with them—but then he knows that he need not imagine it. It is there—or rather, it *was* there—then. So Doctor Lassmann recalls his single playmate Klara, not without effort. Until the day he went to boarding-school, at the age of about ten, he shared with her everything that happened to him, little that it was (or was it much?). Klara had no sisters or brothers, and he had as good as none; for his older sisters did not concern themselves with him. But since then he had never asked anyone about her. How was that possible?—He leaned back. She had been a pious child, he still remembered, and then he asked himself: What can have become of her? For a time the thought frightened him that she might have died. An immeasurable dread overcame him in the closely packed compartment; everything seemed to confirm this assumption: she had been a sickly child, she hadn't been very well off at home, she had often cried; undoubtedly: she is dead. The doctor could not stand it any longer; he disturbed certain of the sleepers, shoving his way between them into the corridor of the car. There he opened a window and gazed out into the blackness with the dancing sparks. That quieted him. And when he returned to the compartment later, despite his uncomfortable position he soon went to sleep.

The reunion with his two married sisters passed off not without embarrassment. The three had forgotten how far apart, notwithstanding their close relationship, they had always remained, and endeavored for a while to act like brother and sisters. However they soon silently agreed to take refuge behind that polite mediate tone which social intercourse has invented for all occasions.

It was at the house of his younger sister, whose husband

was in particularly comfortable circumstances, a manufacturer with the title of Imperial Councilor; and it was after the fourth course at dinner that the doctor asked:

'Tell me, Sophie, what ever became of Klara?'

'Klara who?'

'I don't remember her name. The little one, you know, a neighbor's daughter, with whom I played as a child.'

'Oh, you mean Klara Söllner?'

'Söllner, that's it, Söllner. Now I remember: old Söllner was that awful old man—but what of Klara?'

His sister hesitated. 'She married—and now she lives altogether in retirement.'

'Yes,' murmured the Imperial Councilor, and his knife slid rasping across his plate, 'quite retired.'

'You know her too?' The doctor turned to his brother-in-law.

'Y-ye-es—just slightly; she's pretty well known here, of course.'

Husband and wife exchanged a look of understanding. The doctor noticed that for some reason they did not care to say more on the subject, and he let it drop.

The more eagerness to pursue this theme did the Councilor show when the lady of the house had left them to their coffee.

'This Klara,' he asked with a sly smile, watching the ash that fell from his cigar into a silver bowl, 'wasn't she supposed to be a quiet child, and homely too?'

The doctor said nothing. The Councilor moved confidentially closer.

'That was a story!—Did you never hear of it?'

'But I haven't seen anybody to talk to.'

'Talk to?' the Councilor laughed cunningly. 'You could have read it in the papers.'

'What?' asked the doctor nervously.

'Why, she ran off and left him—' From behind a cloud of smoke the manufacturer discharged this astonishing sentence and waited in unconfined well-being for the effect. But the effect did not seem to please him. He took on a business-like manner, sat up straight and began to report in another, an injured tone, as it were: 'Well, they had married her to Lehr, of the building council. You wouldn't have known him. Not an old man—my age. Rich, thoroughly respectable, you know, thoroughly respectable. She hadn't a penny and in addition she had no looks, no bringing-up, etc. Still, Lehr didn't want a great lady, just a modest housekeeping wife. But Klara—she was taken into society all over, everybody was kindly disposed towards her— really, they acted—well, you know, she could easily have made a position for herself—but Klara, one day—hardly two years after the wedding, off she goes. Can you imagine: gone. Where? To Italy. A little pleasure-trip, not alone, naturally. All that last year we hadn't invited them—as though we had suspected! Lehr, a good friend of mine, a man of honor, a man—'

'And Klara?' the doctor broke in, rising.

'Oh, yes—well, the chastisement of heaven fell upon her. You see, the man in question—an artist, they say, you know—a casual sort of bird, naturally, just—Well, when they got back from Italy, to Munich: good-bye, and she saw him no more. Now she's sitting there with her child!'

Doctor Lassmann strode excitedly up and down: 'In Munich?'

'Yes, in Munich,' replied the Councilor and also rose. 'They say she's having a pretty miserable time—'

'How, miserable?'

'Well,' the Councilor gazed at his cigar, 'pecuniarily, and then anyhow—God, what an existence—'

Suddenly he laid his well-groomed hand on his brother-in-law's shoulder and clucked with pleasure: 'You know they also used to say that she lived on—'

The doctor turned short about and walked out the door. The Councilor, whose hand had fallen from the other's shoulder, needed ten minutes to recover from his astonishment. Then he went in to his wife and said angrily:

'I've always said so, your brother is decidedly queer.'

And she, who had just dozed off, yawned lazily: 'Oh, Lord yes.'

A fortnight later the doctor departed. He knew all at once that he must seek his childhood elsewhere. In the Munich directory he found: Klara Söllner, the name of the suburb, Schwabing, the street and number. He announced his coming and drove out. A slender woman greeted him in a room full of light and kindliness.

'Georg, and you remember me?'

The doctor stood still in amazement. At last he said: 'So this is *you*, Klara.'

She held her calm face with its clear brow quite still, as though she wanted to give him time to recognize her. It took long. Finally the doctor seemed to have found something that proved to him that his old playmate really stood before him. He sought her hand again and pressed it; then slowly let it go and looked about the room. It seemed to contain nothing superfluous. At the window a desk with papers and books, at which Klara must just have been sitting. The chair had been pushed back.

'You were writing?' . . . and the doctor felt how silly the question was.

But Klara answered ingenuously: 'Yes, I'm translating.'

'For publication?'

'Yes,' Klara said simply, 'for a publishing house.'

Georg noticed some Italian photographs on the walls. Among them Giorgione's 'Concert.'

'Are you fond of this?' He stepped nearer to the picture.

'And you?'

'I have never seen the original; it's in Florence, isn't it?'

'In the Pitti. You must go there.'

'For the purpose?'

'For the purpose.' There was a free and simple serenity about her. The doctor was looking thoughtful.

'What's the matter, Georg? Won't you sit down?'

'I've been sorry,' he faltered. 'I thought—but'—and the words escaped him suddenly—'but you aren't in the least miserable—!'

Klara smiled. 'You have heard my story?'

'Yes, that is—'

'Oh,' she interrupted quickly, as she saw his brow darken, 'it's not people's fault if they speak *differently* of it. The things we experience often cannot be expressed, and any one who insists on telling them nevertheless, is bound to make mistakes—' A pause.

And the doctor: 'What has made you so kind?'

'Everything,' she said softly and warmly. 'But why do you say: kind?'

'Because—because you really ought to have grown hard. You were such a weak, helpless child; children of that sort later either grow hard or—'

'Or they die, you mean. Well, I died too. Oh, I died for many years. From the time I last saw you at home, until—' She reached for something from the table. 'See, this is his picture. It flatters him a little. His face is not so clear-cut, but—nicer, simpler. I'll show you our child in a moment, it's asleep in the next room. It's a boy. Called Angelo, like him. He is away now, traveling, far away.'

'And you are all alone?' asked the doctor absently, still absorbed in the photograph.

'Yes, I and the child. Isn't that enough? I will tell you how it is. Angelo is a painter. His name is little known; you would never have heard it. Until lately he had been struggling with the world, with his plans, with himself and with me. Yes, with me too; because for a year I've been begging him to travel. I felt how much he needed it. Once he asked jokingly: "Me or a child?" "A child," said I, and then he went.'

'And when will he be back?'

'When the child can say his name, that's how we arranged it.' The doctor was about to comment, but Klara laughed: 'And as it's a difficult name, it will take a while yet. Angelino won't be two till summer.'

'Extraordinary,' said the doctor.

'What, Georg?'

'How well you understand life. How big you have grown, how young! What have you done with your childhood? We were both such—such helpless children. But that can't be altered or made never to have happened.'

'You mean, we ought to have *suffered* from our childhood, by right?'

'Yes, I mean just that. From that heavy darkness behind us with which we preserve such feeble, vague relations. There comes a time when we have deposited in it all our firstlings, all beginning, all confidence, the seeds of all that which might perhaps some day come to be. And suddenly we realize: All that has sunk in a deep sea, and we don't even know just when. We never noticed it. As though some one were to collect all his money, and buy a feather with it and stick the feather in his hat: whish!—the first breeze will carry it away. Naturally he arrives home without his feather, and nothing remains for him but to look back and think when it could have flown off."

'You are thinking of that, Georg?'

'Not any more. I've given it up. I begin somewhere behind my tenth year, at the point where I stopped praying. The rest doesn't belong to me.'

'And how is it, then, that you have remembered *me?*'

'That is just why I have come to you. You are the only witness to that time. I believed I could find again in you—what I can *not* find in myself. Some gesture, some word, some name that would carry a suggestion—some enlightenment—' The doctor's head sank into his cold, restless hands.

Frau Klara pondered. 'I remember so little of my childhood, as though there were a thousand lives between. But now that you remind me of it so, something comes back to me. One evening. You came to us, unexpectedly; your parents had gone out, to the theater or something of the sort. Our house was all lit up. My father was expecting a guest, a relative, a distant wealthy relative, if I remember rightly. He was coming from, from—I don't know where, but in any case from some distance. We had already been awaiting him for two hours. The doors were open, the lamps were burning, my mother went over from time to time and smoothed an antimacassar on the sofa, my father stood at the window. Nobody dared sit down for fear of displacing a chair. As you happened to come, you waited with us. We children listened at the door. And the later it grew, the more marvelous a guest did we expect. Yes, we even trembled lest he come before he should have attained that last degree of gloriousness to which with every minute of his not-coming he drew nearer. We were not afraid that he might not appear at all; we knew for certain he would come, but we wanted to leave him time to grow great and mighty."

Suddenly the doctor raised his head and said sadly: 'So we both know that—that he *didn't* come. I had not forgotten it either.'

'No,' Klara corroborated, 'he didn't come—' And after a pause: 'But it was lovely all the same!'

'What?'

'Oh, well—the waiting, the many lamps—the stillness —the festive spirit.'

Something stirred in the next room. Frau Klara excused herself for a moment; and as she came brightly and serenely back, she said: 'We can go in now. He's awake and smiling.—But what was it you wanted to say just now?'

'I was just wondering what could have helped you to—to yourself, to this calm possession of yourself. Life certainly hasn't made it easy for you. Evidently something helped you that I haven't got.'

'What should that be, Georg?' Klara sat down beside him.

'It is strange; when I first remembered you again, one night three weeks ago, on the train, I thought: She was a pious child. And now, since I have seen you, although you are so entirely different from what I had expected—in spite of that, and yet, I would almost say, only the more surely, I feel that what led you through all dangers was your—your piety'

'What do you call piety?'

'Well, your relation to God; your love of God, your belief.'

Frau Klara closed her eyes. 'Love of God? Let me think.' The doctor watched her intently. She seemed to speak her thoughts slowly, as they came to her: 'As a child—did I love God? I don't believe so. Why, I never even—it would have seemed to me insane presumption—that isn't the right word—like the worst sin, to think: He is. As though I had thereby compelled him to be *in me*, in that weak child with the absurdly long arms, in our poor apartment where everything was imitation and false, from the bronze wall-plaques of papier mâché to the wine in the bottles that bore such expensive labels. And later—' Klara made a parrying gesture with her hands, and her eyes closed tighter, as though she feared to see something dreadful through the lids—'why, I would have had to drive him out of me if he had been living in me then. But I knew nothing about him. I had quite forgotten him. I had forgotten *everything*.—Not until I came to Florence, when for the first time in my life I saw, heard, felt, realized and simultaneously learned to be thankful for all those things, did I think of him again. There were traces of him everywhere. In all the pictures I found bits of his smile, the bells were still alive with his voice, and on the statues I recognized the imprints of his hands.'

'And you found him there?'

Klara looked at the doctor with large, happy eyes: 'I felt that he *was*—at some time once *was* . . . why should I have felt *more?* That was already more than enough.'

The doctor got up and went to the window. From it one could see a stretch of field and the little old village church of Schwabing, and above it sky, no longer quite untouched by evening. Suddenly Doctor Lassmann asked, without turning round:

'And now?'

Receiving no answer, he came quietly back.

'Now—' Klara faltered as he stood before her, and then raised her eyes full to his face, 'now I sometimes think: He will be.'

The doctor took her hand and kept it a moment. His gaze seemed so abstracted, undefined.

'What are you thinking of, Georg?'

'I'm thinking that it's like that evening once more: *you* are again waiting for the wonderful guest, for God, and know that he will come— And I have joined you by chance—'

Klara rose, calm and happy. She looked very young. 'Well, this time we'll really wait until it happens.' She said it so joyfully and so simply that the doctor had to smile. And so she led him into the adjoining room, to her child.—"

In this story there is nothing that children may not know. Still, the children have *not* heard it. I have told it only to the dark, to no one else. And the children are afraid of the dark, and run away from it, and if some time they have to stay in it, they press their eyes shut and put their fingers in their ears. But for them also the time will come when they love the dark. From it they will learn my story, and then they will understand it better, too.

Notes

ANYONE WORKING on Rilke these days owes an enormous debt of gratitude to the Insel-Verlag's definitive edition of the *Complete Works* (*Sämtliche Werke*) under the able editorship of Dr Ernst Zinn, on which much of the following information is based (here referred to as *EZ*). Grateful acknowledgement is also due to the (English) notes in Dr Eva C. Wunderlich's Upsala College study edition of the *Geschichten vom lieben Gott* (Twayne Publishers, Inc., New York, 1957—here *ECW-1*), especially those covering local customs in Rilke's youth, references to the Renaissance and to Russia (the latter being based on her "Slavonic Traces in Rainer Maria Rilke's *Geschichten vom lieben Gott*" in the Germanic Review, xxii, 4; Dec. 1947, pp. 287–297— here *ECW-2*). Further, Sophie Brutzer's dissertation on *Rilkes russische Reisen* (Albertus-Universität, Königsberg Pr., 1934—here *SB*) which remains a fundamental study of Rilke's Russian experiences; to which we may now add "Letters of R. M. Rilke to Helene Woronin" by V. Voutchik, E. L. Stahl, S. Mitchell (Oxford Slavonic Papers, Vol. IX, 1960, pp. 133–164—here *HW*), and the excellent summary in Part IV of W. L. Graff's *Rainer Maria Rilke—Creative Anguish of a Modern Poet* (Princeton University Press, 1956).

Translator's Note

p. 9   ". . . these youthful fantasies . . .": Letter of January 25th, 1921, to Rudolf Zimmermann, pastor at Berg in Switzerland, where Rilke was then staying.

"fond of this book": for example, the letter to Ellen Key of February 13th, 1903.

p. 10   roundabout approach . . . "something about God": Letter to Friedrich Huch of July 6th, 1902.

"unhandy and unpretty": Letter to Ellen Key of February 6th, 1904.

The alterations: as described by Dr Zinn (*EZ*).

changed his mind . . . "alone with itself": Letter to Ellen Key of April 29th, 1904. The foreword was a fragment of a lecture-essay on Rilke and his work, originally published in the Swedish illustrated monthly *Ord och Bild* (Stockholm, 1904) as "Rainer Maria Rilke. En österrikisk diktare", subsequently included in its German translation as "Ein Gottsucher (Rainer Maria Rilke)" in Ellen Key's *Seelen und Werke* (S. Fischer Verlag, Berlin, 1911).

p. 11   "youthful pre-prose"; Letter of January 26th, 1925, to Anton Kippenberg.

p. 12   his fascination with Russia and her people: "The landscape of the Russian soul corresponds with the landscape of Russia, the same boundlessness, formlessness, reaching out into infinity, breadth." These words might have been Rilke's own. They are those of no less a Russian, religious philosopher and Christian than Nicolas Alexandrovich Berdyaev, who further explains that "In the

typical Russian two elements are always in opposition
—the primitive natural paganism of boundless Russia,
and an Orthodox asceticism received from Byzantium,
a reaching out towards the other world." (*The Origin
of Russian Communism*, Charles Scribner's Sons, New
York, 1937).

p. 13   dealt with elsewhere: Cf. *ECW-1*.

The Tale of the Hands of God

There appears to be some possibility that this story
may have a Ukrainian source, stemming, with differ-
ences, from "a very naïve *Genesis*" written by an
eleventh century monk and to be found in the *Nestor
Chronicle*, a twelfth century anthology of which there
is a French translation of 1884 that may have been avail-
able to Rilke. (*ECW-2*).

p. 18   horse-car: This is the word Rilke uses, *Pferdebahn*.
Readers in this motor-bus age may not recall that in
the early years of the twentieth century the motive
power of street-cars in Europe and the United States
was still the horse. The cars ran in tracks, as the later
electric cars did (and do?) so that the power came in
chiefly for starting and for the rare upgrades.

The Stranger

p. 28   Rilke has a good deal to say about Russian paintings
that impressed him. Among these, two—Nicolas Gay's
confrontation of Christ and Pilate, *What is Truth?*,
and Kramskoi's *Derision of Christ by Herod*[*ias?*]—

have given rise to the suggestion that the figure of the stranger in this tale represents the dark (Russian) Christ "who wanders over the earth unrecognized and persecuted and yet can never be extinguished; from the deep glow of his gaze something says that he is the one 'eternally coming' ". (*SB.*)

How Treason Came to Russia

p. 39   For likely sources of this story, which Rilke may have known in Russian or in a French translation, cf. *ECW-2*.

p. 42   *bylina:* a legendary tale or poem, from *byl*, an event or past occurrence, derived from the past of the verb to be, *byt'*. (The accent falls on the second syllable, and the *y* represents not our y but the dark, throaty i-sound of the seventh vowel of Russian, for which we have no equivalent.)

p. 43   Vassily the Naked: The great church of many fantastic towers in the Red Square, built by Ivan the Terrible (1533–1584) and known as Vassily the Blessed, or Cathedral of the Protector or the Patron. Basil (Vassily) the Great, or Saint Basil (c. 330–379), one of the famous Cappadocian Church Fathers, a man of strong personality, "both sensitive and pugnacious", was responsible for establishing the standards of Eastern monachism introduced into Russia by Basilian monks in the eleventh century. He believed in chastity and poverty but did not favor the extremes to which certain hermits were given. If Rilke calls him "the Naked", which, after all, is often synonymous with very poor, he may (as *ECW-1* suggests) have been following the *bylini* in this use of the word.

How Old Timofei Died Singing

p. 49   *skaski:* plural of *skaska,* a tale, story, in this case folk-tale.

p. 51   Diuk Stepanovitch: a Ukrainian hero.

The Song of Justice

p. 55   "Both among the Russian masses and among the Russian intelligentsia will be found the search for a kingdom founded on justice. In the visible kingdom injustice reigns. In the Muscovite kingdom . . . . was mingled the Kingdom of Christ, a kingdom of justice, with ideas of a mighty state ruling by injustice. . . ." Again Berdyaev (*loc. cit.*)

p. 56   the Iberian Madonna in Moscow: the *Panaghia Portaïtissa* (Virgin of the Gate) in the Iberian Gate of the Red Square, a copy of the original miraculous icon in the Iviron (= Iberian = Georgian) monastery on Mount Athos, about whose beneficent influence there are many stories. It is deeply venerated; it has even been said to be one of the three "known" paintings by Saint Luke. In 1648 Tsar Alexis Mikhailovitch, very ill, urgently requested the monks of Iviron to let him have it; instead they sent him a carefully executed copy by the iconographer Jamvlichos Romanos. In thanks the Tsar presented Iviron with the monastery of Saint Nicholas at Moscow. (E. Amand de Mendieta, *Le Mont Athos,* Éd. Desclée de Brouwer, 1955). This author says it almost requires an act of faith to see the drops of blood upon her neck, so blackened with time; but "the eyes of the *Panaghia Portaïtissa* are gentle and dreamy."

133

Baedeker's *Russia* (4th and 5th German editions, of 1897 and 1901, respectively) describes how the icon is "driven almost daily around the streets of Moscow by six horses and bareheaded liveried footmen, reverentially greeted by the people, the sick, at family celebrations, etc. It is then borne through all the rooms of the house and, after receiving some compensation in money . . . drives on to some other family that has asked for its visit." (*EZ*)

In July 1899 Rilke had been reading Lermontov's poem, *Demon*, which put him in mind of Russia, of the idea that there pride and humility are one:
"Before the little Iverskaya chapel in Moscow: there those who kneel are bigger than those who are standing, and those who bow down stand up gigantic: thus it is in Russia." (*HW:* Letter of July 27th).

p. 59　keys of the churches: In their exploitation of the Ukraine the Poles gave the Jews charge of opening church doors against payment of a tax which they then turned over to their masters. (*ECW-1*).

p. 62　the Setch, to the Zaporozhian Cossacks: The *Zaporozhskaya Setch* (also transliterated Syetch, Sech, Sich, and by Rilke misspelled Ssetch), a famous community of Cossacks settled beyond (below) the falls or rapids (*porozh*) of the Dnieper on islands in the river and hence called Backfallsmen or Trans-Rapids Cossacks; they were originally regiments trained for defense of the region against Tatar invasions.

p. 62　'Ostap!': a historic character of the nineteenth century, Ostap Mikitin Veresai, one of the last kobzars and blind, whom Rilke for his own purposes here places in a much earlier period.

p. 63   kobzars: players of the *kobza*, an early, widely-played
lute-like instrument, originally with two strings, later
with four to eight pairs. (The reproduction in *ECW-1*
of V. M. Vaznetsov's painting of three "Blind Kobzars"
shows the instrument lying across the seated singers'
knees, as would be the case with our own 3-stringed
Kentucky mountain dulcimer.) By the sixteenth century it had been completely replaced by the *bandura*,
which would appear to be the instrument Rilke describes, having 6 strings strung along the fingerboard,
plucked with a plectrum, and 6 sympathetic strings next
them along the body. It became a very popular folk instrument, especially among the Ukrainian Cossacks.
Some thirty years ago it might still be met with in small
villages, and in the hands of blind players. (Riemann,
Musiklexikon, 1929).

p. 63   hetmans: elected chiefs or headmen of the Cossacks. Of
those here named the third is the hero of the famous
Russian novel, *Taras Bulba*, by Gogol, whose own
father was a Zaporozhian Cossack official.

p. 63   Znamenskaya: a much-painted icon, the *Znamenie Pres-*
viatoi Bogoroditzy (Apparition of the Most Holy
Mother of God), presumably the one in the Znamenskaya chapel of the monastery of the same name in
Moscow. Later in the letter of July 27th, 1899, quoted
above, Rilke tells his correspondent that when he knows
the language he will feel "wholly Russian. Then will
I bow down before the Znamenskaya, low, three times
and in the orthodox way." (*HW*). All this Madonna
interest of Rilke's may have had an early start, for over
the door of his grandparents' house in the Herrengasse
in Prag—a house he often speaks of—hung a Madonna
with a perpetual light before it, and this his mother had

removed when the house was sold, later bringing it to the little church of Saint Anne, just above his tower of Muzot, which Rilke in celebration of his fiftieth birthday undertook to have restored. (Carl Sieber, *René Rilke*, Insel-Verlag, 1932).

p. 63   Ostranitza and Nalivaiko: Ukrainian heroes.

p. 64   The Song of Justice: Whatever the source on which Rilke drew for his version of this Ukrainian elegiac poem, he here translates *pravda*, truth, in its secondary meaning, justice. In the story of how treason came to Russia he has the church-building peasant say that he needs not gold but "truth and justice", thus giving the word both meanings. His verses, rhymed, as were those of the original Slavonic, paraphrase only a part of this old song, which was recited by Ostap Mikitin Veresai himself at the archeological congress in St. Petersburg in 1874 and subsequently published. (*ECW-2*)

p. 64   little mother . . . wing that is like to the eagle's: This apparently irrelevant combination of images may be explained by the fact that the Slavonic version implies that *pravda* is to be had only with one's mother, truth being addressed as "O you eagle-mother", while "later in the poem the kobzar wished for eagle-wings in order to fly to truth." (*ECW-2*).

A Scene from the Ghetto in Venice

p. 67   a small bird: In German primers there is a story of a boy who could not doff his hat properly because he had sparrows hidden under it. (*ECW-1*).

p. 68   '*Dove?*': 'Where?'

p. 70 'Sensa': (abbreviation for *Ascenzione*) the historical ceremony held on Ascension Day [and last held in 1728–(*ECW-1*)], known as the "Marriage of the Sea", in which the Doge from his galley threw a gold ring into the Adriatic, symbolizing Venetian domination over that sea.

Of One Who Listened to the Stones

p. 77 Pietà: One should perhaps not try to relate Rilke's description to a specific statue (neither of Michelangelo's Pietàs being a completely finished work); it may be his own way of conveying what the sculptor might be imagining.

p. 77 Julius della Rovere: Julius II (Giuliano della Rovere) pope from 1503 to 1513, commissioned Michelangelo to make him a great sepulchral monument, which was never finished save in the sculptor's old age in a much changed and much smaller form. Three of the proposed figures with which it was to be "peopled", however, completed between 1513 and 1516, are among Michelangelo's finest works: the famous *Moses* in S. Pietro in Vincoli in Rome and the two *Slave* figures in the Louvre.

How the Thimble Came to Be God

p. 83 Pythagorean proposition: It might help those of us likely to find ourselves in the same position as the boy's mother to be reminded that in right-angle triangles the square on the hypotenuse is equal to the sum of the squares on the sides (which we should have learned from Euclid, I, 47).

A Society Sprung of an Urgent Need

p. 97   Flagfather: a literal translation of *Fahnenvater*, the word Rilke uses. Much as we would christen a regimental flag, it was a custom in Austrian clubs at the time of Rilke's youth for a member to act as godfather (a woman would play godmother) at the ceremony to inaugurate the club's flag. (*ECW-1*).

The Beggar and the Proud Young Lady

p. 110   Not to leave the verse at a translation from a translation, here are Rilke's lines:

> *Wie schön ist die Jugend, die uns erfreut,*
> *Doch wer will sie halten? Sie flieht und bereut,*
> *Und wenn einer fröhlich sein will, der sei's heut,*
> *Und für morgen ist keine Gewissheit.*

Rilke's delight in the personality of Lorenzo de' Medici, from whose *Canti* the verse is taken, is charmingly described in his Tuscan diary of the Spring of 1898 (*Briefe und Tagebücher aus der Frühzeit*, Insel-Verlag, 1942, pp. 46–47, 64, 67.—EZ). He there quotes (pp. 110–111) the Italian lines:

> *Quant' è bella giovinezza*
> *che si fugge tuttavia.*
> *Chi vuol' esser lieto, sia!*
> *Di doman non c'è certezza.*

which might be literally translated:

How beautiful is youth
though it be ever fleeing.
Who would be happy, let him!
Of tomorrow there is no certainty.

A Story Told to The Dark

p. 120 Schwabing: a suburb of the old pre-World War II
Munich in which many professional people and artists
lived.

p. 125 ". . . in our poor apartment where everything was
imitation and false: . .": Among objects "in the bad
taste of the '70s" inherited by Rilke's mother and sur-
rounding him in his early years, there were, besides
many Japanese fans and knick-knacks of all sorts, forty
pictures set in red plush with views of Vesuvius, Arco,
and sundry saints hanging on the walls; and, regretting
the enforced modesty of her domestic set-up, this
strange lady of whom we hear so little and so much
would, for parties, arrange to paste high-sounding vin-
tage labels on bottles containing some simple table
wine. (Carl Sieber, *loc. cit.*).